POISON SHY

POISON
SHY

STACEY
MADDEN

MISFIT

ECW PRESS

Published by ECW Press
2120 Queen Street East, Suite 200, Toronto, Ontario, Canada M4E 1E2
416-694-3348 / info@ecwpress.com

LIBRARY AND ARCHIVES CANADA CATALOGUING IN PUBLICATION

Madden, Stacey, 1982–
Poison shy : a novel / Stacey Madden.

ISBN 978-1-77041-075-6
ALSO ISSUED AS: 978-1-77090-286-2 (PDF); 978-1-77090-287-9 (EPUB)

I. Title.

PS8626.A314P63 2012   C813'.6   C2012-902687-5

Editor for the press: Michael Holmes / a misfit Book
Cover design: Dave Gee
Cover image: i.m. ruzz
Interior image: The black silhouette of a bedbug © lantapix / Shutterstock
Type: Troy Cunningham
Printing: Trigraphik   5   4   3   2   1

The publication of *Poison Shy* has been generously supported by the Canada Council for the Arts which last year invested $20.1 million in writing and publishing throughout Canada, and by the Ontario Arts Council, an agency of the Government of Ontario. We also acknowledge the financial support of the Government of Canada through the Canada Book Fund for our publishing activities, and the contribution of the Government of Ontario through the Ontario Book Publishing Tax Credit. The marketing of this book was made possible with the support of the Ontario Media Development Corporation.

PRINTED AND BOUND IN CANADA

To the memory of Robert Brown

My worst fear? Insanity. All the different kinds of crazy.

Paranoid, psychotic, deranged.

Homicidal.

It's not so much being insane that scares me as the prolonged descent, degree by fractured degree, into the cavern of madness. Not the oblivious haze of the landing place but the horror of the journey. The creeping awareness of your own mental disintegration.

My name is Brandon Galloway. I don't have a middle name. I grew up in a place called Frayne, a blue-collar nowheresville in southwestern Ontario. Aside from being an open sanctuary

POISON SHY

for addicts, drunks, and aging prostitutes, it's also a college town — home to Frayne University, which the students devotedly refer to as F.U.

A vine-wrapped, yellow-stone behemoth that looks like a giant birdhouse with tentacles, F.U. is a place for students with average grades and parents who can't afford to send them elsewhere. Some say it's the pride of the town, a symbol of respectability. I say it's a red herring: nothing but a small-town sham.

When the university was founded in 1964, it split Frayne into two halves: right and wrong. The red-brick and white-picket-fence homes on the residential east side comfort the teachers, aldermen, and small business owners, while the rubbled tenements of the west shelter the steel worker and janitor types, along with the unemployed, the forgotten, and the ignored. The dividing line is a long bustling road called Dormant Street, the aptly named downtown core, where the students lie oblivious to the simmering poverty of the west and the taken-for-granted entitlement of the east, until life sees fit to kick or hoist them in either direction. Or until they leave town, like I did.

These days, whenever someone learns I'm a Fraynian by birth, I can almost hear their thoughts. They wonder if I was involved in the kidnapping of Melanie Blaxley or the murder of Darcy Sands. It was the only time my hometown made the national news.

I tell them I wasn't involved. But I was.

I didn't have the happiest childhood, but I was an adaptable kid. Mostly I was invisible, hovering in the background of my parents' smash-up derby marriage, a mere afterthought in their battle of emotional attrition.

My father worked as an electrical technician. He moved in and out of our home more times than I can remember. He was the kind of man who could fuck a waitress at a motel in the afternoon, then snore in my mother's bed at night with an undisturbed conscience. On his forty-first birthday he suffered a heart attack in a strip club bathroom and died. He wasn't living with us at the time.

My mother started showing signs of schizophrenia in her mid-twenties, and was finally diagnosed after Dad's death. His philandering didn't help. My mother was prone to bouts of violent jealousy. Somehow I always knew she was crazy, even before I knew what crazy was, though it didn't affect my love for her. It's common to love and fear something at the same time. Religious fanaticism is a prime example of this phenomenon, and my mother was one of those, too — a fanatic, that is. Schizophrenics cling to religion because they believe everything on earth is out to get them, and in many ways they're right. The world is hostile and everything in it clashes. My mother and father were about as suitable for each other as a nun and a gangster. It often made me question the legitimacy of my existence.

At school I sat at the back of the classroom, blending into the coat rack with an ashen complexion and earth-tone clothing. I was the student the teachers always had trouble remembering, a receiver of mediocre but unworrying grades. I once achieved a 72% in a class I'd stopped attending months before the end of term. "A valiant effort" was what the teacher wrote on my report card.

I wasn't picked on because the bullies didn't know who I was. I won the "participant" ribbon at the school track meet, finished eighth runner-up at the science fair, and signed out library books with fake names and never got caught. The flying pudding cups and bologna sandwiches of cafeteria food fights always seemed to miss me.

After school I'd go straight home, close my bedroom curtains, and get lost in a video game with the volume turned down. I didn't want my mother to know I was home; otherwise I'd have to sit through a Bible lesson.

When I grew bored of blowing away zombies, I'd peep out my window and invent life stories for the neighbourhood passersby. My seventh-grade teacher, Mr. Zettler, was a government agent working undercover. Patricia Moreno, my neighbour and classmate, was the descendent of an ancient Mayan emperor with supernatural powers. The garbageman with the eye patch was secretly writing an adventure novel that would one day make him rich. I heaped fame and fortune onto strangers but gave no thought to my own hopes and dreams. I was a comfortable nobody. I spent my youth watching the world and hoped it wouldn't notice I was a part of it. My primary concern was security, and my means of achieving it were simple. *Stay out of sight and out of trouble* became my personal motto. I believed I'd found the secret to longevity, and I shared it with nobody.

By the time I finished high school, however, I'd grown tired of being a spectator. I enrolled at F.U. and applied for student housing. I wanted to break out of my solitude and get involved in something social, like the Drama Society or the Athletics Club. It didn't take me long to discover that all the drama geeks were pretentious assholes, and that most of the vein-pulsing jocks were closet homosexuals who fucked sorority girls for sport and secretly pined for each other in the locker room shower. It wasn't something I wanted to be a part of.

After another year of average grades, no friends, and a

loneliness gloomier than the one I'd felt in high school, I moved out of my dorm and dropped out of school entirely. I spent my days that summer hanging around the public library, reading horror novels in the mornings and scouring the want ads in the afternoons. I worked as a pizza delivery guy, a telemarketer, a grocery bagger, a dog walker, and endured two whole shifts as a clerk at a stationery store before being fired for doing crossword puzzles behind the check-out counter.

Finally, I settled for a dishwashing gig at a bar near campus called The Place. Eventually I worked my way onto the kitchen staff, preparing mayo-thick Caesar salads and brushing suicide sauce on Buffalo wings. I earned minimum wage, plus a small percentage from the collective tip jar and a doggy bag of leftovers at the end of every shift.

Patricia Moreno, my childhood neighbour, was one of the servers. In just a few years she'd transformed from a long-eyelashed pre-teen into a chubby sex-bomb, forever doomed to wax her upper lip. A spicy Latina who could flirt with the customers with her hips alone, she was the only other staffer my age, so we spent a lot of time together. Eventually, almost without my even noticing, we became a couple.

I couldn't tell you how long we dated. The start and end points of our relationship were too vague and tranquilized to be assigned firm dates. We came together out of convenience, but remained emotionally detached. It was strictly business at work, board games and movie rentals on our mutual days off.

In the beginning we spent a good amount of time in bed, but once we got used to each other's kinks (she liked to be held down, I liked to do it standing up), we pretty much stopped fucking altogether. She refused to have sex on Sundays (the Lord's day) or anytime after work ("My feet stink, Brandon. Are you crazy?"), which pretty much left no time at all. Her parents hated me because I couldn't speak Spanish, or even French. To them I was just another Canadian-born kid with no ambition and hockey on the brain (which was only half-true — I've never been much of a sports guy).

She confirmed the break-up I long suspected over the phone. She called from a bus station in Montreal, said she'd gone to start a new life. She'd been plotting her escape for months.

I mourned her departure with a basket of chicken fingers and three shots of tequila. What upset me wasn't that she'd left, but that she'd managed to take a risk and actually *do something* before I had.

At this point I'd been working at The Place for seven years, the ones I'd been told are supposed to be the best of your life. I lived alone in a small apartment above a twenty-four-hour laundromat, slept on a soggy mattress that folded up inside a couch. On my days off I'd fall asleep with my hand in a bag of Cheetos and a dog-eared Stephen King on my chest, only to be ripped from my slumber by the shaking and buzzing of the dryers downstairs. I had no savings, no hobbies, and no friends to speak of besides an ex-jock from my old high school named Chad Baldelli. He'd been kicked off the football team at McMaster after suffering three concussions in his freshman year. He came into The Place at least three times a week and bored the flies off the walls with his endless musings on what might've been, before being helped into a cab at three a.m., drunk as a donkey and weeping into his empty wallet. I felt for the guy. I loaned him my ear a couple of times, and before I could remind him that we'd never actually spoken in high school, he'd latched onto me like a virus.

"Yo, bartender! A brewski for me, and one for my best buddy here!"

More than once he suggested we hit up a strip joint in

Toronto, or at least a sleazy nightclub — "Where the girls get drunk and dance with their asses hanging out."

I'd shirk the topic and bring up Patricia.

"You're living in the past, dude. Come out with me and I'll introduce you to some honeys that'll make you forget all about her."

Chad quickly became my only friend, not that I ever took him up on his offer to go "snatch hunting." He brought me out with him once or twice, and invited along a few old flames from his glory days — ex-cheerleaders who were now either waitresses, nannies, or cashiers at the Stop N' Save — no one interesting enough to lure me into reliving the passionless sitcom of my previous relationship. Even Chad's antics, which had distracted me for a while, were starting to get old. I needed a change, something to help me figure out who — or what — I was.

Then something remarkable happened. A few weeks after Patricia left, like some divine mercy, The Place was shut down after a rat infestation. I heard the exterminator say it was the worst he'd seen in his twelve years on the job.

Twelve years killing vermin. The thought struck me as poetically macho. Sad and noble at the same time, not to mention secure. It wasn't like insects or rats were going extinct anytime soon.

I wrote up a resumé and dropped it off. Within the week I was called for an interview. By sheer luck they'd just had three employees leave for higher-paying extermination jobs in Toronto. Despite my lack of experience I was hired on the spot. I was told I had the eyebrows of a bug killer, which I took as a compliment.

I shook the man's sandpapery hand and waited for him to ferret out a uniform from the maze of boxes in the back room.

I first saw Melanie Blaxley the day I fumigated her apartment. I'd been working as a junior exterminator for Kill 'Em All Pest Control for a few solid months. My supervisor was a guy named Bill Barber. He was fortyish, unmarried, overweight — exactly what you'd expect of your neighbourhood bug guy. A friendly blue-collar slob. I was the one who looked out of place.

Melanie was a student, living in a shabby two-bedroom apartment with her roommate, Darcy Sands. Their problem was bedbugs. I remember standing on the sidewalk outside their building, waiting for Darcy to clear out. Melanie was sharing a cigarette with Bill. She was a redhead, pale and freckled, with eyes so icy green they resembled the stick of spearmint gum I'd just popped into my mouth. She wore a low-cut purple top that speared down between her small breasts and a frayed pair of cut-off jean shorts with a bleach stain on the ass. Small, scabby bites ran up her legs from her ankles to her thighs. It was early October and the weather was mild.

She must have caught me staring, because when she finished her cigarette, she flicked it in my direction. It landed inches from my shoe. For some reason I had the urge to bend down and pick it up. I didn't smoke and never have, but Melanie had left a smooch of lip gloss on the filter and I wanted to know what it tasted like.

Darcy came slouching out of the apartment as I fought the urge to pick up the butt. He had five or six enormous text-books in his hands. He looked pissed.

"This is *not* a great time for a fumigation, you know," he spat. "I have a philosophy paper due and now I'll have to write it at the goddamn library."

At the time, I assumed he was talking to Melanie. But thinking back, it's possible he was talking to me and Bill. Or himself. Or nobody at all.

"You guys got everything you need?" Bill asked them. He attempted to hike up his pants despite his enormous gut. "Once we start you can't go back in for at least twenty-four hours."

"Wonderful," Darcy said. "Looks like I'll be checking into a cubicle tonight."

"Hey, we gave you notice —" I said, but Melanie cut me off.

"It's okay, he knows. He's just being an asshole."

I looked directly into her face for the first time. She gave me a crooked smile, which could just as easily have been a smirk of contempt. There was something distinctly feline about her. A subtle predatory glint in those green eyes of hers. The freckles suited her. They seemed to be scattered symmetrically across her face, the same minute distance between each spot with not a single one out of place. She was beautiful in a trashy kind of way. I imagined her as the surprisingly attractive offspring from an incestuous marriage.

"What about you?" I asked her. "Do you have a place to stay?"

She laughed as if she was mocking and forgiving me at the same time. "Yeah, I got it covered."

I stood and watched her walk down the street with Darcy. She took a few textbooks out of his hands to share the load. He tried to trip her, but she swerved to avoid his foot and whacked him playfully on the shoulder. As they turned the corner, Melanie doubled over laughing at something Darcy had said. It was ridiculous, but I felt they were joking around about *me*. I also felt there was more to their relationship than just splitting the rent.

But all of this is hindsight. At the time, their closeness bothered me because I was attracted to her, and Darcy was biological competition.

"You coming, Brandon?" my supervisor called from the building's front steps.

"Yeah, sorry Bill." I spat my gum onto the curb and followed, the bottles of bug spray on my belt clanking like tin cans.

My mother was still alive at this time.

She was a recluse, shut away in her tiny apartment, only venturing out when the government shot laser beams through her window to intercept her thoughts. She had this disgusting woollen blanket she kept wrapped around herself at all times

— when she ate, when she slept, when she went to the bathroom. It was Halloween orange and smelled like it had been pulled out of a dumpster. It was encrusted with food stains, boogers, and God knows what else — she never washed it. For her, it was literally a security blanket, some kind of signal-muffling force field that kept her safe from harm.

Whenever those government lasers came beaming through her windows, usually between three and five a.m., she'd burst into the hall, donning her blanket like a cloak, and begin banging on her neighbours' doors, cursing like a lunatic. She was the filthy woman with the wild hair, the blanketed zombie in 33C who gave all the kids nightmares.

"Why in the world would the government want access to your thoughts?" I asked her on one of those rare occasions I felt bold enough to challenge her conspiracy theories.

She looked at me and held up a veiny, trembling hand. "If I told you, then you'd be in danger, Brandon." She hacked up some phlegm and spat into the bucket at her feet. "They never target the target. They're very cunning. They go after your loved ones. That's how they violate your soul."

I wanted to vomit at the thought of someone I loved being so far gone. I was filling her fridge with groceries at the time, so she didn't see me shudder. All the teenagers I'd tried to hire as grocery boys had quit. She'd scared them away with volcanic prophecies of doom and death. In the end I had to do the shopping myself, but I didn't mind. It gave me an excuse to visit, and I think she was grateful for the company.

One time, while I was organizing soup cans by brand — she was meticulous about this for some reason — she said, "I saw the woman drunken with the blood of the saints."

I turned to look. Her gaze was fixed on the TV screen. She

was watching one of those televised religious services on mute. An old man in a purple robe lifted his hands toward the stained glass above his head.

"Are you talking to me, Ma?"

"Hmm?"

"You said something about a drunk woman . . ."

"I did?"

"You just said it, Ma."

She stared at me blankly. "I must have been talking to Jesus."

I shook my head, my heart crumbling a little at what she'd become. It's only now I can see that she was giving me some kind of warning, whether she knew it or not.

A good chunk of my paycheque went to booze. I was twenty-nine and single with a decent job and very few living expenses. My apartment above the laundromat was rent controlled. I ate a lot of fast food: macaroni, veggies and dip, canned soup, peanut butter and jelly — your basic bachelor's diet.

Chad was my sole drinking buddy. His rediscovered lust for women had helped him forget about his sporting fame that never was. He liked them tall and full-figured, with big asses and saggy bell-clapper breasts. A girl who could touch her nipple to her belly button drove Chad wild. No matter where we went, he always seemed to find a girl who just happened to be into meatheads with out-of-control chest hair.

I wasn't so lucky. My approach to meeting women was essentially a non-approach. I liked to sit back, make eye contact, smile, and wait for them to come to me. It didn't work every time — in fact it rarely worked. Most nights I was left to wander home alone after Chad had helped his soon-to-be conquest into a cab. I didn't mind, really; there was always Internet porn, one hundred percent STD-free.

Chad's favourite bars were what I call plush holes — dimly lit date joints with high tables and cushioned stools that served ice wine and raspberry-flavoured beer. I couldn't stand them. He said he went for the bimbos. I went because I didn't have any other friends.

One night, I told Chad I was in the mood for something different. We went to this new place called The Bloody Paw I'd read about in *The Frayne Exchange*. According to the article, the bar's owner was an environmentalist named Viktor Lozowsky. He'd spent the last few years in the Northwest Territories, canvassing for a save-the-bears project he'd spearheaded, and had recently returned to the place where he'd grown up. He'd decorated the walls of his establishment with graphic hunting photos — animal carcasses, live bears caught in various traps, beavers being skinned alive. He said he wanted to expose his customers to the horrors of animal cruelty, and shock them into taking political action.

The strategy struck me as more perverse than inspiring, but the thought of spending another night watching Chad caress the bronzed thighs and glittered shoulders of the barely legal daughters of Frayne was enough to make me insist on The Bloody Paw.

We showed up during peak hours of campus pub life. A gathering of smokers puffed and mumbled on the sidewalk outside the bar. A scruffy guy with a harelip opened his mouth to show his pierced tongue to a gaggle of tipsy blondes.

"Guaranteed to moisten you up and put you in a trance," he said to them.

Chad and I snaked our way through the crowd to the

entrance. Once my eyes adjusted to the dim orange lighting, I saw the place was packed with all manner of college dweebs in pre-ripped jeans, second-hand T-shirts, and oversized sunglasses. They slouched over the checkerboard tables, watered-down pints and mixed drinks in hand, and discussed the teenification of punk rock and Hemingway's sexual orientation with straight faces and unbrushed teeth. The music of Neutral Milk Hotel crashed through the speakers and sank down into the funk of patchouli oil, stale beer, and armpit reek.

The photos decorating the walls *were* explicit. In one, a massive grizzly roared at the camera as he tried to pull his blood-caked paw from a trap's teeth. In another, the same bear lay dead on its side, its eyes black and dead as a stuffed toy's. Inches from its head was an upturned chunk of skull. Bits of brain hung over the rim like stew. The third photo in the sequence showed an older man with his arm around a younger man's shoulder. The younger man held a shotgun. The bear lay in the background like a lump of dirt.

Chad made a barfing sound with his throat. "Come on, let's grab a table."

We'd had two or three beers before I caught a glimpse of a freckled face at an L-shaped table in the corner. Melanie Blaxley sat with ten or fifteen others, all of them clapping and cheering on a broad-shouldered guy with thick-rimmed glasses and a shaved head. He stood on his chair and took a bow. His mouth was moving like he was giving a speech, but the music was too loud to hear anything. Also at the table was Melanie's roommate Darcy. Seeing his matted hair and yellow, watery eyes again gave me the creeps.

"What's going on over there, you think?" I asked Chad.

"Not sure," he said. "But I think that guy might be the owner. That wacko you were telling me about."

"Really? How come?"

"Well, I don't know. I'm guessing. I overheard someone at the table behind us say he's Viktor something-or-other."

"Viktor Lozowsky, yeah."

"What a nutjob."

I watched him for a while as he gabbed and gestured like some enthused orator. His friends seemed to eat up everything he said, Melanie included. Darcy was the only one who looked like he didn't give a damn.

I couldn't stop staring at Melanie. Her hair was pulled tight behind a thin black headband. Her top was low-cut and hung open between her breasts. I wanted to shrink myself down, climb onto the bendy straw in her drink, and dive head-first into her cleavage.

"That chick's hot," Chad said, nodding in Melanie's direction.

"Tell me about it."

"You should go talk to her, man. I know you like to play Mr. Cool, but listen: if you don't go talk to her, I will." He sat back in his chair and crossed his arms.

"Come on, Chad. She's with a big group of friends. Any one of those guys could be her boyfriend."

"No way of knowing unless you talk to her," he said, which was bullshit. There were plenty of other ways to find that out. Patient observation, for one. But I knew Chad was going to keep on my case until I did something.

"All right. Fine." I gulped down the rest of my beer. "I'm going to embarrass myself, and it'll be your fault."

He rubbed his hands together.

I'll admit that part of me *did* want to talk to Melanie. I just wasn't prepared. It occurred to me that what I passed off as a tactic for meeting women was really just shyness and self-doubt. I racked my brain for an excuse to talk to her. Perhaps she'd remember me from the fumigation. I could ask her quickly about the results, then hurry back to my table and tell Chad that I'd been right about her having a boyfriend.

Nobody noticed me coming as I made my way slowly to her table. When I was almost there, Melanie stood up. Darcy stood up as well and went to her side. I stopped and waited. They made their way together to the bathrooms. Melanie whispered something in Darcy's ear that made him laugh, and then Darcy put his hand inside the back pocket of Melanie's jeans. His knuckles clenched and squeezed her ass. He kept his hand inside her pocket until they reached the door to the ladies' room and Melanie went inside.

Well, there's my answer, I thought.

I turned around and there was Chad, chatting up a chubby, olive-skinned girl in a red poncho. Her large rear end was in my seat. It hadn't been more than thirty seconds since I'd stood up.

"Oh, Brandon, this is Farah," Chad said. "She's from Lebanon." He raised and lowered his eyebrows, as though this were impressive information.

"Nice to meet you." I turned to Chad. "I think I'm going to take off. Enjoy yourself." I tossed him a twenty-dollar bill.

He said, "Brandon, man, wait," but I just walked out.

The image of Darcy's hand in Melanie's back pocket burned inside my eyelids. As I made my way home, I imagined them fucking in their stuffy, bug-ridden apartment. Why Darcy? Maybe Melanie was one of those girls with inexplicably low self-esteem. Maybe she was in a phase of claiming that looks weren't important to her, and purposely sought out an unattractive mate in order to prove her point. Maybe Darcy had saved her from a near-death experience. Maybe he was rich, or grotesquely well endowed. I tortured myself with increasingly ludicrous scenarios. Darcy was a vampire, a were-wolf. Satan himself.

It was after midnight when I got back to my place. I stripped down to my boxers, made myself a sandwich, and sat in front of the television. I put on the sports channel, turned the volume down low, and converted my pull-out couch to bed mode. I tried reading a book, some Dean Koontz best-seller, but I couldn't get Melanie out of my head. I went to the kitchen and opened the fridge. Stared mindlessly at a jar of pickles and a carton of milk. My copy of *The Frayne Exchange* was open on the kitchen table. I sat down and flipped to the back pages, to the section advertising escorts and prostitutes.

I came across a redhead named Suzie. The photo showed her bent over a chair with her face blurred out, two black stars over her nipples. I told myself that when the clock on the micro-wave changed, I would have to make a decision: call or don't.

12:37 became 12:38. I picked up my phone and dialled the number. It rang three or four times then a woman said, "Hello?" The voice was hoarse, like Kirstie Alley's.

I was silent. My mind was blank.

"Hello?" the woman asked again, a little louder.

"Yes, hi. Sorry. Is this, umm . . . Suzie?"

"It sure is. And who is this?"

"This is, uh, Darcy."

"Nice to hear from you, Darcy. You don't have to be shy. It's all right. I'm friendly, see? You've woken me up and I don't mind. Are you looking for a date, honey?"

I admitted that I was and gave her my address. She said she'd be over in half an hour, she just needed to shower. I tried not to think about what that could mean.

After precisely half an hour — I'd been watching the clock — Suzie still hadn't shown up. I opened a beer and drank it down in three or four big gulps. I felt the stirrings of panic in the back of my skull. It occurred to me that I should call her back and cancel.

As soon as I picked up the phone, however, someone buzzed my apartment.

"Yeah?" I said into the intercom, trying to sound both casual and confident.

"Is this Darcy's place?"

I pinched my eyes shut. It was difficult to remain standing, to support my own body weight. "Uh, yes it is. Is this Suzie?"

"It sure is, honey. You wanna buzz me in?"

I thought about throwing on some pants and a T-shirt as I waited for her to come up the stairs, but decided it didn't matter. I'd just hired a prostitute for the first time in my life. Did I really need to be concerned about making a decent impression?

She reached the top of the stairs and knocked. I could smell her perfume through the door. I swept all my doubts into some far-off, cobwebbed corner of my conscience and turned the handle, half-expecting to be confronted by my father's ghost, or Medusa, or Jesus Christ Himself. Instead I saw a woman with curly red hair and large freckled breasts that were straining to burst out of her little black dress. She smiled at me with a mouth covered in red lipstick. A layer of wrinkles appeared at the corners of her eyes.

"Hey there." She stepped inside, heels clicking on the hardwood floor. Her mauve-painted toenails were cracked and unusually long. She looked me up and down. "You look like you're ready to get down to business."

She looked to be in her early fifties. Older than I expected, but I was so full of alcohol, so pathetically horny, that I found myself obscenely attracted to the idea of fucking her.

POISON SHY

She asked for the money up front. Eighty bucks, a bit lower than I had thought. She slipped out of her dress and exposed her enormous, water-balloon breasts. Her thighs were full of bruises and cellulite, her kneecaps covered in scabs. She performed oral sex on me while I sat on my mattress and stared blankly at an infomercial for a vacuum cleaner with state-of-the-art sucking technology. I tried to conjure up a mental image of Melanie's face, but it kept morphing into Patricia's — the only other face I'd ever seen between my legs. I stared up at the ceiling and concentrated on finishing the job as quickly as possible.

When we were done, she asked to use my bathroom. I could hear her vomiting into the toilet. She came out reeking of perfume and handed me her business card, a shot of her much younger self straddling a stripper pole. I watched out my window as she got into a cab and drove off to wherever.

I felt dirty. I felt alone. I opened a bottle of whisky and drank myself to sleep.

I never paid much attention to clients' households. Whatever mess they left lying around — dirty laundry, credit card statements, pornography — my job was to come in, wipe out whatever vermin was making their lives miserable, and leave. There was no judgment involved, no snooping around. No scoffing at old family portraits or clever rearrangement of fridge magnets. The private lives of Frayne were about as interesting to me as the breeding habits of the common crayfish.

One time, when I was working with a guy named Ansel, we were called in to take care of a cockroach problem at the apartment of one of our frequent clients, Gottfried Burl. Mr. Burl was the owner of a breakfast diner called Egg on Yo' Face. It had been featured on one of those restaurant makeover reality shows, and became an overnight success as a result. Kill 'Em All had a deal going with Mr. Burl: we sent him free rat traps in exchange for half-price takeout for all KEA employees.

None of us had ever been to Mr. Burl's home before. Ansel and I figured it was no big deal. We met him outside his building. He gave us the keys, said he was heading to Vancouver for a weekend "rendezvous." We let ourselves into his apartment, and honest to God, the guy had swastikas all over the place. I mean *everywhere*. On the walls, on the lampshades, on the floor tiles. He even had a framed portrait of Adolf Hitler in his living room. It was like walking into a miniature Nazi museum.

I remember the expression on poor Ansel's face — sheer bewilderment. He was Jewish. I can only imagine how he must have felt, standing in that place in his mustard-brown uniform, a dented can of bug spray hanging at his waist like a gun. I remember thinking: if I were him, I'd trash the place. But Ansel was one of the most mild-mannered guys I've ever known. I told him he didn't have to stay, and after his shock wore off, he took me up on it and left. I finished the job myself, suppressing the urge to poison the food in Mr. Burl's fridge.

A week later, Ansel quit. I didn't blame him. He and his girlfriend moved into her parents' place in some suburb of Toronto. A few days after that, rumour got around that Mr. Burl had been shot and killed in a church basement poker game out west. His restaurant was turned over to his sister, and our rat-traps-for-takeout deal came to an end. I never told my boss what I saw in Mr. Burl's apartment, and I don't think Ansel did either. It was sort of an unwritten rule in the pest control business that we turn a blind eye to our clients' lives, no matter how troubling or strange — or alluring.

That rule was on my mind the next morning as I lay in bed, thinking about the fumigation at Melanie's apartment. I'd snooped around a bit. I hadn't been able to resist.

"Just gonna use the bathroom," Bill had said, as soon as we stepped inside. "That pastrami sandwich isn't agreeing with me." He hustled down the hallway, keys jingling.

"Take your time."

The place was small. Cozy. There was something distinctly masculine about it: posters on the wall for *Pulp Fiction* and *The Shining*, empty beer cans on the duct-taped coffee table. A TV plunked on a sagging milk crate. An Xbox and a small pile of video games on the floor. Curtains fashioned out of faded bedsheets. An old sweatshirt slung over a lampshade. A mountain of unwashed dishes in the sink.

I could hear Bill grunting away in the bathroom, the spillage of his guts. I knew I had more time to look around, so I made my way to the bedrooms down the hall.

The first door I came to had a No Exit sign nailed to it. Written below the sign in black marker was the phrase *The truth is rarely pure and never simple* — Oscar Wilde's words, though I didn't know that at the time. I did know, right away, that this was Darcy's room. It smelled of wet dog and masturbation. The mess was similar to the one in the living room: two empty beer cans on the nightstand, dirty socks and underwear on the floor. Something resembling a cross had been crudely spray-painted on the wall above the crusty futon bed.

Across the hall was a plain white door. It was closed. I put my hand on the knob. My palms were moist. I bit my lip and entered.

Melanie's room smelled of sharp cloves and candle wax. The walls were painted a deep blue and had been decorated with an intricate collage of Polaroid photographs. One of the pictures showed Melanie in a thin white tube top and red short shorts. She held a cigarette in one hand and a half-drunk bottle of vodka in the other. She was walking along the seat of a park bench as though it were a tightrope. Her eyes were pinched shut and her mouth was wide open: an ecstatic scream, frozen in silence. The full moon shone directly over her head like a halo turned on its side. It was one photo among hundreds overlapping on the wall. I plucked it off and stuffed it in the back pocket of my uniform.

There was a heap of laundry on the floor, and another on the unmade bed. Some of the clothes looked like they could have been Darcy's, but it was hard to tell. On a small desk in the corner was a laptop, and above that, a vintage *Playboy* calendar. October's playmate was a petite brunette in cut-off jean shorts, stretched out topless on a bale of hay.

I looked at what Melanie had written on some of the dates.

October second: *Jill's 21ˢᵗ b-day*

October fifteenth: *American Lit essay due*

October thirty-first: *Halloween, bitches!*

The toilet flushed. I scrambled back into the hallway. Bill emerged from the bathroom. I caught a throat-clenching whiff of shit mixed with air freshener.

"Jesus," Bill said, fanning the air with his hand. "You think the bugs are already dead?" He laughed in a fit of wheezes. His self-deprecating jolliness made the stench more bearable, and I laughed along with him.

We put on our masks and sprayed the living room and kitchen before moving on to the bedrooms. Bill went straight for Melanie's room, so I got stuck with Darcy's. Wrestling his multi-stained futon into the plastic case was one of the more unpleasant experiences of my life. The side of my hand touched a stain that still felt wet.

I blocked it out and thought about Melanie. I wondered how old she was and where she'd grown up. Was she an only child like me? Were her parents alive? Did she have any bad habits or outrageous childhood dreams? I thought about taking her out to dinner, bombarding her with questions. Spotting constellations in her freckles. Would it be considered inappropriate to ask her out on a date?

My father had met my mother while rewiring her parents' two-bedroom home in London, Ontario. He was twenty-five at the time, she eighteen. According to the story I was told as a child, my father was down on his hands and knees in the upstairs hallway, examining a faulty outlet, when my mother came out of her bedroom in her nightgown without her glasses on. She was near-blind without them. On her way to the bathroom, she stumbled over my father and nearly broke her back. She said she fell in love with him in that instant, but I know that's just a simplification of things, the way the stories of our lives get pared down over time into these condensed and delusive versions of the truth.

Did the story of my parents' meeting influence my desire for Melanie in any way? It's possible. If so it was unconscious. It's funny how our parents can manoeuvre us into disastrous scenarios without even trying — sometimes without even being alive.

I'm not so naïve as to think my parents didn't have problems before I grew old enough to start noticing them. My mother was a religious fanatic and my father was a hedonistic drunk.

Problems were inevitable. The sad thing is that these kinds of inexplicable unions are all too common, born of the clichéd notion that opposites attract. Maybe they do, but truisms are rarely conducive to happiness.

There was no watershed moment at which our family orb shattered into bits. It was more like a gradual splintering, each argument adding new chips and cracks with the force of a foot stomp.

The night of my tenth birthday stands out as one of the more damaging blows. My father hadn't been home for five consecutive days. I was afraid to ask my mother where he was because I didn't want my question to seem like a reminder or an accusation. She was doing a good job of pretending everything was normal, so I just went along with it.

I was in my bedroom playing video games when she came and stood in the doorway.

"Do you want me to take you to the mall?" she asked.

I paused my game and looked at her. There was violence stirring in her eyes. They seemed to quiver in their sockets. It was the first time I felt unsafe in her presence. I learned at a young age that my parents weren't the steady, reliable safeguards I'd once imagined them to be. Instead they were frail, selfish, and vengeful — just like everyone else.

"Okay," I said, only because I didn't want to make matters worse.

While we shopped, my mother scanned the board games and stuffed animals like they were relics from another universe, touching them delicately with her fingers as though they might crumble into powder. She responded to everything I said with a vacant "Hmm?"

I showed her an expensive action figure I wanted. She'd refused to buy it for me a number of times before because it came with a small plastic rifle that shot real pellets. This time, she agreed to buy it without a fuss.

"I'm putting this on your father's credit card," she said while we were standing in line. I had no idea why she would tell me that. I didn't know what credit cards were for.

When we arrived back home, my father's car was in the driveway. I thought my mother would be relieved, but she muttered "Fucking asshole" as we went up the walk. It made me want to stay outside, but for some reason I didn't.

My father sat with his legs crossed at the kitchen table, a cigarette clenched between his teeth in the centre of his mouth. He seemed different to me somehow, as if my memories of him from before his disappearance were of another man with the same face. He reached down into the plastic bag at his feet and pulled out the same action figure my mother had just bought me.

I looked at my mother for some indication of what to do.

"Go to your room, Brandon, okay? Mommy and Daddy need to talk."

I went to leave, but my father had other ideas.

"Don't go anygoddamnwhere." He exhaled two tusks of smoke. "What's the matter? You don't like your toy?"

"Brandon." My mother's voice. "Go to your room."

I didn't move.

My father got down onto one knee in front of me. He rested his elbow on his thigh and leaned forward. There was a circular burn mark on his forearm. He smelled like a bucket of old rain. He reached out, put his hand on my shoulder, and squeezed. "Happy birthday, little man."

I'm not sure how it happened — I didn't even feel it happen — but as he knelt there in front of me, breathing smoke in my face, I pissed my pants.

POISON SHY

The next thing I remember is my mother leading me upstairs to the bathroom.

"Why don't you have a hot bath?" she said, shaking. "I'll have to wash those pants."

I stood in the doorway and watched her go back downstairs. When the yelling started I bolted inside the bathroom, locked the door behind me, and sat in the tub with the shower curtain drawn. Both of them were shouting over each other. I didn't hear the words, only wails and growls, raging human voices in combat. Fists pounding tabletops, dishes smashing. Feet thumping across the floor.

I crept out later and heard my mother cry, "No, Jack, no! Please no!" I had this image of my father breaking off my mother's limbs one by one with his bare hands, then tossing them into a pile at his feet.

I sat nervously at the top of the stairs. My father stomped toward the front door, holding a bloodstained dishtowel to his head. My mother darted after him and clawed the sleeve of his shirt, tearing it at the shoulder.

"Jack, please!"

He swatted her away with the bloody rag. There was a dark, pulpy gash above his ear. He swung the front door open and walked across the lawn to his car. My mother grasped at him with her fingernails, screaming his name, hysterical.

I don't remember coming down the stairs, but I must have. I watched them from the front doorway. I hated what I saw but couldn't look away.

My father got into his car and slammed the door, missing my mother's hand by inches. He started the engine and peeled out of the driveway. My mother ran barefoot onto the road after him. I thought my father would drive off and leave her alone in the middle of the road to scream into the dusk. Instead he let the car idle and revved the engine, his face a dark blur behind the tinted window. My mother grabbed the door handle and tugged on it frantically, using her full body weight in a series of violent jerks. She looked like someone being electrocuted.

Even as my father started pulling away she wouldn't let go. Her bare feet slapped on the pavement as she ran alongside the moving vehicle. The car picked up speed. My mother's legs flailed wildly. When she finally let go of the handle, she tumbled forward, scraping her knees, hands, and face on the road.

One of our neighbours had come out of his house. He approached my mother and helped her to her feet. Her face was scratched up but her eyes were calm. She dismissed her helper with a wave of her hand. I looked around at the faces in the windows on our street. They were all focused on my mother as she walked numbly back to our house, the corners of her mouth twisting into a smile.

In my whisky-soaked sleep I had a dream I was sitting in a fishing boat on a lake of black water. The sky was orange and smeared with sharp red clouds. Everything was still until something splashed behind me. I turned and saw Melanie treading water about twenty feet from my boat. She appeared to be naked. I stared at the pattern of freckles on her shoulders and collarbone that led down between her breasts. She lowered her head to the lake and slurped a mouthful of water until her cheeks were full, then spouted it in my direction.

"Hey," I said, reaching for the oars in my boat. "Wait!"

She turned and started swimming away, moving through the water at dolphin speed. It was then that I saw her sparkling green mermaid's tail, the same colour as her eyes.

"Wait!" I said again.

POISON SHY

She was far away now. There was no hope of catching her. I set down the oars and just watched her. A shark lunged out of the water. Its protruding jaw resembled a rusty metal bear trap. The shark sank its teeth into Melanie's torso, ripping her in half. Blood and scales exploded in all directions. Clumps of flesh and cracked bone landed centimetres from my boat.

I woke to my telephone ringing. I squinted at my alarm clock. 6:31 a.m. I wormed out of bed and checked the call display. It was Chad. He probably wanted to brag about the sex he'd had, or was about to have, or was in the middle of having, with whatever her name was.

I yanked the phone cord out of the socket and went back to my sweaty sheets.

After a few hours of half-sleep I plugged the phone back in and called in sick.

It was a Friday, and Fridays were always busy in the pest control business. The weekend provided an excuse for people to get out of town while their homes were being filled with poison. I plugged my nose with a clothespin and hacked violently into the receiver as I fed my boss a story of fever and cold sweats. I'm not sure he bought it, but it didn't matter. I couldn't handle a day of sweeping up insect and rat carcasses after the night I'd had.

I made a pot of coffee and drank it black, sipping on it mechanically as I watched the morning news. Apparently the citizens of Frayne were getting fed up with people driving up from Toronto to dump their garbage, due to a sanitary workers' strike in the city. I thought of the rats and the maggots, all that disease. It made me glad I didn't work in Toronto. The next story involved a local politician who was suspected of having ties to a prostitution ring. I thought about Suzie and her bruised legs, and wondered if I should get tested for STDs. God knows how many men she'd been with — hundreds, maybe thousands of scabby johns.

I dug my fingertips deep into my eye sockets. "Fuck me," I moaned.

Just then my phone rang. It was Chad again. This time I picked up.

"You took off so suddenly last night," he blurted. "What the fuck? Anyway, you missed one hell of a night! Farah's the coolest chick ever."

I grumbled.

"What's the matter, B-Dawg? You hungover? Did you sneak off last night with that redhead?"

I held my finger against my temple like a gun. "No."

"Some other broad, huh? That's cool. Anyway, the reason I'm calling is to tell you that Farah and I made plans again for tonight. Is it okay if you and I take the night off? I was going to leave a message 'cause I thought you'd be at work. You must've had more fun last night than I thought!"

I cleared my throat. "Listen, Chad. I've got a massive headache. I need to get off the phone. But you and Farah have fun tonight, okay?"

"Oh, we will. Don't worry about that! We've had plenty of fun already, if you know what I mean. She's got an ass on her the size of Brazil! I'm talkin' . . . just, wow! And she's a sweet girl, too. Smart, funny, soft-spoken. Only thing is, her old man's a cop. I better be careful with this one, eh?" He laughed. "Anyway, take care of that headache, dude, all right?"

I hung up the phone feeling worse than before. I wanted to get out of my apartment and thought about visiting my mother, but I needed to calm my own nerves before subjecting myself to hers. I decided to go for a walk. I filled my thermos with the rest of the whisky and a splash of ginger ale, grabbed an orange, and set out for nowhere in particular.

It was warm for late October, though a bit grey. I walked through the parkette down the block, past a huddle of dog owners. Their beasts scampered about, barking and pawing and inhaling each other's assholes, revelling in their daily tease of freedom. I lurched past them like a homeless vampire. A Jack Russell terrier approached me and yapped, wagging its nub of a tail like a disapproving finger. I belched at it and carried on.

I wandered eastward into the nicer part of town, a sub-urban oasis in the middle of a concrete wasteland. White picket fences, immaculate lawns, fake plastic window shutters, that whole fairy tale. I could only imagine the domestic night-mares concealed behind those wholesome facades. Childhood memories began to stir. I swallowed some whisky and wound my way back downtown to Dormant Street.

I was riding a nice buzz but I needed to go to the bathroom. I looked around for a pub or fast food joint where I could pee anonymously without having to be a customer. There was a scuzzy-looking place across the street called Burgers. It would do. I slipped past a table of drug addicts, playing checkers in the corner, and ducked into a door marked *Gentlemen*.

It was one of the most decrepit public toilets I've ever seen. Against the stucco wall was a single urinal that no longer had a bottom. It looked like it had been smashed with a cinder block. There was a puddle of urine on the floor amidst the broken

POISON SHY

ceramic debris. I leaped over the pond of piss, entered the only stall that wasn't sealed shut with duct tape, and flushed the reeking heap of filth and cigarette butts that lingered in the bowl.

"Lord," I muttered as I unzipped my fly.

Holding my breath, I perused the graffiti scribbled above the toilet.

> *Looking 4 a hoodsuck? Athletic twink wants to swallow*
> *your cock!*
> *Meet here October 15, 8:30 p.m. SHARP*

I checked my watch in a brief moment of panic. It was only 3:41 p.m. I exhaled and felt the shiver up my spine subside as I finished my business.

I'd seen that date marked somewhere else recently. It came to me as I washed my hands: Melanie had an essay due on the fifteenth. She'd marked it on her *Playboy* calendar. She seemed like the kind of student who'd throw a half-assed paper together at the last minute in a caffeinated frenzy. I imagined her typing it at the library, naked and winking at her voyeuristic schoolmates. The thought gave me a hard-on. I tucked it under the elastic waistband of my boxer shorts and walked out into the grey late afternoon.

Hungover, I scoured the outskirts of campus for a girl I didn't know, spurred on by whisky and the male instinct to hunt, even to stalk. I peered through the window of every coffee shop, pub, and Internet café I passed. I was blind to the judgmental gaze of the student body, only one thing on my mind.

By the time I arrived at the campus library I'd been walking for close to an hour. The temperature was starting to drop. I sat down on a concrete bench outside and blew on my hands. A man in glasses and a sweater vest hurried past me, clutching a briefcase to his chest, and ran up the steps to the library doors. As he reached for the handle, the door swung open in front of him, and out burst Darcy Sands in an old leather jacket. They slammed into each other. Sweater Vest dropped his briefcase, the buckles popped open, and a flurry of papers spilled all over the steps.

"I'm so sorry!" Sweater Vest said. He bent down to gather his things.

"Watch where you're going!" Darcy spat. "Fuck!"

I pulled some change out of my pocket and pretended to count it, hiding my face from view. Darcy zoomed past me playing air-drums. I didn't know whether to follow him or to see if Melanie was inside the library. I opted for the latter.

And there she was, right in the front, hunched over a laptop at a cubicle next to the info desk.

I could tell it was her from the back. She was wearing a thin white tank top and low-rise jeans, exposing masses of freckles on her shoulders, arms, and lower back. She turned around to look at the clock on the wall behind her and didn't notice me.

I sat down at a nearby study table and took the orange out of my pocket. My heart was beating in my throat, my fingertips. I peeled the orange and stared at her, placing the bits of rind in a little pile. She ran a hand through her hair and sighed. I watched her every movement like a camouflaged predator. My nerves were somehow both numb and broiling — I felt stiff and robotic, yet ready to pounce. Who did I think I was? I felt like a criminal, uncomfortable in my own lust-hungry skin. For all I knew, she'd turn around, see me, and scream. The campus police would swarm into the library and swoop down on me, tasers and truncheons in hand.

"Excuse me, sir?" said a voice from behind.

They've caught me, I thought, sniffed me out. I turned and readied myself to be escorted off the premises.

A middle-aged little person in a blue and white dress stood in front of me like something out of *The Wizard of Oz*. There was a badge pinned to her chest that read *Ask me for assistance*. "There's no food allowed in the Information Commons," she said.

"I'm sorry. I didn't realize."

"There's a lounge upstairs where eating is permitted."

"Great." I stood up. Melanie had turned around. She was looking straight at me and squinting, as though trying to remember where she recognized me from.

I dropped my orange on the floor. She laughed. My insides withered. I picked up the orange and scrambled upstairs to the lounge. Why didn't I just leave? I had no reason to be there. I'd been patrolling the campus in search of some other guy's girlfriend, and now that I'd found her, what did I expect?

I sat down on one of the cold pleather couches and picked carpet fibres off my orange. There was a sign on the wall that read *Thank you for keeping the library clean*.

When Melanie came up the stairs I was in the middle of scraping a small hair off my tongue.

"Hey," she said and sat down on the couch across from me. She placed her folded laptop beside her and pulled a brown paper bag out of her backpack.

"Hey."

"I saw you get in trouble downstairs, and it reminded me I haven't eaten a thing all day. Stupid essay."

I smiled and nodded like the biggest fucking numbskull on the planet.

She took out a sandwich. "I know you from somewhere. Are you in my art history seminar? I haven't been to that class in forever. Prof smells like cat litter."

I cleared my throat. "No, actually, I'm not a student here." I stuffed another dusty piece of orange in my mouth and stared at the carpet.

"I think I saw some lint on that orange slice."

I had just swallowed it. "Oh."

She bit into her sandwich. It smelled like tuna. With her mouth full, she said, "Okay, really. Where do I know you from?"

Was her memory that bad, or was I as forgettable as a face in a waiting room? I already knew the answer. I realized it didn't matter what I said. I was nobody to her. Strangely, the thought helped me relax.

"You don't remember? My colleague and I are responsible for ridding your apartment of vermin. Bedbugs, I believe." I cringed at the sound of my own voice, the affected tone of self-importance.

"Oh, *yeah*. I knew I recognized you."

"So is everything okay, or . . . ?"

"Totally. It was mostly my roommate's bed that was the problem but it's all good now. I haven't had a bite since." She pulled up the leg of her jeans to show me the proof.

I pondered her use of the word *roommate*.

"What are you doing at the library?" she asked. "You weren't stalking me, were you?"

I swallowed the wad in my throat. "I came to get a book, actually."

"Oh yeah? With whose student card, Mr. Exterminator?"

She was teasing me. And she'd caught me in a lie. It was incredibly sexy.

"Believe it or not, I was planning on stealing it," I said. "What's it to the university? An insurance write-off, that's what. If they even notice it's gone."

She gave me a sly look. "Very true."

"Any recommendations?"

"Nope. Books are for nerds and grannies. I only read what I have to for school, and usually not even then."

There was something tomboyish and vulgar about her. She sat with her legs spread apart, smacking away on her sandwich. There were crumbs all over her lap and she wasn't wearing a bra.

"Listen," she said. "If you really want to steal a book, be my guest. I won't tell. But if you don't feel like being a criminal I'll let you use my student card. It's the least I can do for a bug-murdering hero like you."

"Really?"

"For sure. What's your name, anyway?"

"Brandon Galloway."

"I like Mr. Exterminator better. I'm Melanie. And I'm not telling you my last name because you're a stranger."

"Fair enough."

She took one last bite of her tuna and stood up. "Go get a book and come find me when you're done. I have to finish this fucking essay. And no naughty books, perv."

I watched her go back downstairs, tossed the remains of my fuzzy orange into a wastebasket, and headed for the stacks.

It was impossible to make sense of the way the books were arranged. I was used to the public library with its boldfaced headings: *HISTORY, PSYCHOLOGY, FICTION*. Here I found myself stonewalled in section PR35766.6B. There were books on literary theory, psychoanalysis, and semiotics, with a few first-hand accounts of the Korean War thrown in for good measure, probably by someone as lost as I was.

No wonder academics have trouble functioning in the real world. My father used to say that the university was nothing more than a glorified dating service, a means of social networking for those who couldn't get a date in high school. In turn, the students with blue-collar destinies could enter the workforce while their so-called smarter peers were herded up and sent away to write meaningless theoretical papers and cultivate their sense of moral superiority.

I watched the passing tide of people for a few minutes. A group of students gathered in front of a laptop and howled with laughter at a clip of a chimp sticking its finger up its ass and sniffing it. A couple who looked like they might have been twins sucked each other's faces behind a book trolley. A guy in a football jersey promised his friend top marks as he photocopied the stolen answers to their Sociology exam. A pink-haired hipster unzipped his fly and stuck his hand in his pants while perusing a volume of Renaissance art. A bearded professor scribbled something onto the forearm of a giggling blonde. Maybe my father was right.

I did my best to ignore these tableaux and headed back downstairs, abandoning my search for a book. Something told me that choosing nothing would impress Melanie more.

I found her planted in front of her laptop, leaning forward as she typed, her low-rise jeans exposing the pinched curve of her butt crack.

I crept up behind her. "Working hard?"

"Holy shit, you scared me!"

"Sorry."

Someone at another workstation shushed us. "Oh fuck off," Melanie whispered loudly. She turned to me. "Watch my laptop for two seconds? I gotta take a shit."

As she made her way past the check-out counter, I snuck a look at her computer screen. She'd chosen to write on Hawthorne's *The Scarlet Letter*.

*The A on Hester Prynne's shirt doesn't stand for America
or Adultery, it stands for Anarchy. Hester can be seen as
a 17th century revolutionary. She disregarded the laws
of 'common decency' and raised Pearl out of wedlock.
It was her fuck you salute to the oppressive morality of
the U.S. of Assholes.*

The whole thing smacked of unfounded self-righteousness
and false moral indignation. I couldn't imagine she'd come up
with any of this drivel on her own. She'd likely tricked some
geek into helping her — probably someone a lot like me.

"Don't read it, it sucks," she said from behind me.

"No, it's —"

"Couldn't find a book, eh? I don't blame you. The books in
this place are, like, from a different time. Anyway, here." She
handed me a little slip of paper with something written on it.

"Send me an email. We'll have a drink or something. My
friend just opened a new bar, it's awesome. You're not gay, are
you?"

"Huh? No."

"Good. Now if you'll excuse me, I really have to get this
stupid essay done."

We were shushed again, by more than one person this time.

"Jesus fuck!" Melanie hissed. She smiled at me.

"I guess I'll talk to you later," I said.

"Great. Now go kill roaches or something."

The sun had just set; the sky was a patchwork of pink and
grey. I took in a lungful of October air. It tasted of cider and
dying leaves. I couldn't remember the last time I'd been in

a genuinely good mood. I pulled Melanie's note out of my pocket and read it again:

Looks like your stalking paid off.
ginger_sex_kitten@sparkmail.net

She was a firecracker all right.

On my way home I went by the grocery store to get some things for my mother. I filled my cart with all her favourites: oatmeal, romaine lettuce, red and yellow peppers, peameal bacon, Earl Grey tea, crackers and cheese, cherry tomatoes, blueberry muffins, thinly shaved roast beef. I stuffed my face with candy and dried fruit from the bulk section and remembered to tell the cashier to add it to my bill.

Outside my mother's building, a toothless man was sitting on the steps. He nodded at the bags in my hand. "Any filet mignon in there, buddy?" he sluiced. Spittle flew everywhere. I dropped a loonie into his gummed coffee cup and went inside.

She wasn't answering her buzzer, so I swooped through the second door as someone was leaving and took the stairs to the third floor. The hallway was dark and empty, which was normal. Still, something seemed wrong.

I knocked. "Mom, you in there? It's Brandon."

No answer.

Something cracked under my shoes. There were bits of broken glass on the rug. "I brought some groceries. Are you there, Ma?"

A soft rustling. I knew the sound: Bible paper.

I tried the doorknob. It was locked. "Let me in, Ma. It's Brandon."

"Upon her forehead was a name written," she said out of

nowhere. *"Mystery, Babylon the great, the mother of harlots and abominations of the earth!"*

I banged on the door. "Mother, stop shouting and let me in!"

Silence.

I sat down at the far end of the hallway and rubbed my temples. After a few deep breaths I heard the door unlock. I tried the knob again and this time it turned. Opened the door slowly. My mother was sitting on the floor in her orange blanket, surrounded by shards of broken dinner plates. She held a rosary in her hands. I wanted to be sick.

"Jesus."

My mother looked up, wide-eyed, and nodded. "Yes. Yes, that's right. And she was drunk with the blood of the saints, and with the blood of the martyrs of Jesus."

I placed the groceries on a clean part of the floor and went to her. "You can't do this, Mom. You can't. Your neighbours have probably called the police."

She touched my arm. Her hand was freezing.

"You've got to wash this blanket."

She said, "I'm hungry."

"Well that's good, because I just brought you some food. Is there a broom in here?"

She gestured toward the kitchen closet.

As I swept, my mother whispered the rosary. I wondered what had spooked her. Probably nothing, and it was too risky to ask. After a fit, it sometimes took her days to calm down.

I made a salad and we ate it together in silence. We watched *Wheel of Fortune*, *Jeopardy!*, and the first half of *Strangers on a Train* before my mother fell asleep on the couch, drooling onto her blanket.

I found a sleeping bag in her closet and rolled it out on the floor.

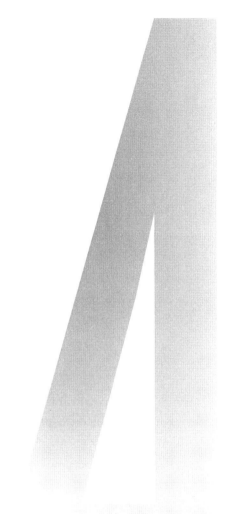

I woke with a stiff neck. My mother was still asleep. I left a packet of oatmeal and a blueberry muffin on her kitchen table. Gave her a kiss on the forehead and got the hell out.

On my way home I stopped at a coffee place called Darryl's Doughnuts. I needed to caffeinate, fill my stomach with sugar. The place was full of senior citizens, all men. They were giving the teenaged girl behind the counter a hard time.

"What d'ya mean you don't have a boyfriend? I bet yer daddy has to beat 'em off with a stick!"

I walked up to the counter and crashed their party. The buzzards looked at me with envy. I was young, healthy. A

POISON
SHY

reminder of everything life had stolen from them. I ordered a large coffee and an apple fritter, then took a seat in the corner, though not far enough away to escape their glowering.

I pulled Melanie's note out of my pocket.

ginger_sex_kitten@sparkmail.net

I had to laugh. She'd dotted her i's with little hearts too, which in her hand seemed ironic and a little nasty.

Did I have any business emailing her? What about Darcy? Was he her boyfriend or just a roommate? No matter how hard I tried, I couldn't see Darcy as gay, and Melanie was definitely the kind of girl who got around. Did I really want to be a part of that quagmire? My nuts cried yes. My brain was a tad more skeptical.

There was a clatter and splash at the other end of the shop. One of the old men had spilled his coffee all over himself and the floor. The girl came out from behind the counter with a mop and poked the old man in the shoulder.

"You've got the shakes, Jack," she said. "You gonna quit drinking, or do I need to get your wife on your case?"

"Are you kidding? Last thing she wants me to do is quit drinking. The sooner I take a dirt nap the sooner she cashes in the insurance policy!"

His friends burst out laughing while the girl mopped. They gripped their mug handles and stared at her like scrawny, aging wolves. The man called Jack nudged his friend as the girl bent over to mop under the table. He gestured as if to squeeze her buttocks; his friend nodded in a spasm of agreement.

It got me thinking about the first time my father took me to his favourite pub. I was twelve, and my father had been living at home with my mother and me for a few months. We went to a place called The Jug off the side of the highway, just outside of Frayne. I knew even then that my father had other women in his life. I think my mother knew as well, but I suppose she was willing to ignore it so long as he stuck around. Horrible as he was to her, his presence seemed to stabilize things. My mother scared me when my father was off living one of his other lives. She'd talk openly to me about demons, about the betrayal of Jesus, about suicide. I'd wake in the middle of the night to hear her reading from the Bible to nobody. Her hands were crosshatched with cuts from accidentally breaking dishes in the sink. I came home from school one day to find she'd gutted one of my stuffed animals. She thought it was possessed.

All these things stopped when my father was home. He'd fill the house with cigarette smoke, spend all night drinking in front of the TV, complain about my mother's cooking, threaten to sell me to the neighbours if I misbehaved. But the fear he inspired made my mother act less insane, and gave me some semblance of security.

The night my father took me with him to The Jug, my mother was staying overnight at the hospital recovering from a tubal ligation. I was glad when I learned it meant she'd no longer be able to have children. I wanted our family to remain intact, just the three of us. I took her operation as a sign of solidarity.

My father didn't say a word to me on the drive to the pub. We listened to the radio the whole way. Weather, traffic, hockey scores. I picked at my cuticles and counted the number of times the host said the word ice.

The Jug was a typical roadside dive: pool tables, dartboards, weekly fist fights in the parking lot. Its menu consisted mostly of dishes with alcohol in the recipe — drunken mussels, beer-battered fish and chips, Irish stout pie. My father wasn't much of an eater. He went for the cheap booze and the cheaper women.

It was dark inside. Half the bulbs in the place were burnt out. The ones that still worked were dusted with dead insects.

My father sat me down at a booth, ordered me a ginger ale and a plate of hash browns, and left me alone with a deck of cards, telling me to play solitaire. He took a seat at a table with a few electrician buddies I'd never met before.

I played a few games and tried not to listen to my father's conversations. Every now and then I'd hear a word or a phrase that scared me, things like "pussy-whipped," "the smell of her twat," and "I broke the bottle right over that cocksucker's bald head!"

The waitress was a woman named Gloria. She had long, sandy blond hair and sunburnt skin, kind eyes and skinny legs. The men in the bar were either shouting at her to refill their beer glasses or drunkenly pleading with her to let them take her home. I watched her play along, fascinated by her ability to control these brutes with a simple nudge of her hip or pat on the back. She noticed me watching and brought over a piece of chocolate cake.

"On the house," she said, and winked at me.

My father ignored Gloria for the most part, which I found strange. My mother had filled my head with so many stories about my father's womanizing that I was stunned by his lack of interest. I wondered if he'd adjusted his behaviour for my benefit. It also occurred to me that my mother might be wrong about him, that her suspicions were a symptom of her deteriorating mind.

Later that night, after the bar had cleared out and I'd long since fallen asleep in my booth, I awoke to someone nudging my shoulder. It was my father. He breathed a stream of smoke in my face and said, "Time to go."

I sat up and rubbed my eyes. I had to think for a moment to remember where I was. My father swung his car keys on his finger, his coat already on. Gloria was waiting by the door.

"It's late, Brandon," said my father. "Let's go."

I followed them to the car. I was groggy and my stomach hurt from the chocolate cake. I looked out the window at the passing blur and tried to figure out where we were going. My father was driving fast. Was my mother in trouble at the hospital? Did Gloria need to be somewhere? Did they plan on killing me and disposing of my body in a field?

We drove into a town I didn't recognize. Looking out the window I saw a man in a red toque asleep on a mat of flattened cardboard boxes. I saw a black girl waiting at a bus stop in pink short shorts, ashing her cigarette into an empty Coke can. I saw a pit bull chained to a parking meter, barking into the darkness. I saw a small L-shaped building, the word *Vacancy* in neon green out front.

We pulled into the parking lot. My father got out of the car. Gloria turned to me from the passenger seat. "You awake?"

I nodded.

"Poor guy. You must be exhausted. Well, don't worry. You'll be in a nice warm bed very soon."

My father came back to the car with two rusty keys in his hand. Gloria and I followed him to a door marked 9. I shivered as he struggled to fit the key into the lock. Once he'd managed to open the door, I went inside, expecting the two of them to follow me. Instead they stood in the doorway. Gloria reached inside and flicked on a light switch.

"Call my room if you need anything," my father said. "Number ten. Just dial 1-0 on the phone. I'll come in and wake you up in the morning."

"All right."

"Sweet dreams, honey," Gloria said.

My father shut the door. There was a spider on the back of it, crawling toward the ceiling where it had made its web.

POISON SHY

I looked at the king-size bed and wondered what was lurking under the faded brown bedspread. I went into the bathroom. It smelled like urine. There was a dead mouse in the shower. I thought about leaving and trying to find my way home, but it was freezing. I had no idea where I was.

I sat down on the edge of the bed and took off my shoes. The mattress was cold and hard as a cinder block. I propped the pillows up against the headboard and lay on top of the sheets. I could hear my father and Gloria talking to each other through the wall. Before long I heard the rhythmic squeaking of bedsprings. I flipped on the TV and turned the volume up full blast. The last thing I remember before falling asleep was an image on the late-night news of a woman being handcuffed for slitting her cheating husband's throat with a box-cutter.

I finished my doughnut shop coffee and went back to my apartment. I slurped down a bowl of Mr. Noodles and descended into the kind of sleep I needed — long, deep, and dreamless. When I awoke two hours later, my answering machine was flashing.

"Hey Brandon, what's up, bro? It's Chad. Listen. Give me a call if you're up for coming out tonight. Farah and I were thinking about hitting up The Bleeding Bear, or whatever it is. Apparently it's half-price wings on Saturdays. What what!"

I hit erase and sat in front of my computer. I hadn't used it in months. I wrote my initials into the dust on the screen as I waited for it to start up. An alert informed me that my hard drive was riddled with viruses. I closed the warning, along with a few pop-up ads for penis enlargement and debt consolidation, and signed into the Kill 'Em All email account I never had reason to use. The only message in my inbox was a memo about Ansel's farewell party from the previous year.

I pulled out Melanie's email address.

Identity: b_galloway@kea.com
To: ginger_sex_kitten@sparkmail.net
Cc:
Bcc:
Subject: hey

Hey Melanie. It's Brandon (aka Mr. Exterminator) from the library. How's it going? I'd like to take you up on your offer to have a drink but I just wanted to ask — are you single? Awkward question, I know, but I don't want to step on anyone's toes. If you are, I'd LOVE to get together. Let me know. Brandon.

PS: You looked great the other day!

I made a turkey sandwich and had a shower. When I came back to the computer there was a message in my inbox.

Identity: ginger_sex_kitten@sparkmail.net
To: b_galloway@kea.com
Cc:
Bcc:
Subject: re: hey

No boyfriend. Chillax, dude. Are you free Thursday night? No class on Fridays, woohoo! I plan on getting smashed. You should join me. Bloody Paw, 10 pm. Be there or be retarded. Mel.

ps: yur gay

I zeroed in on "No boyfriend." Had I imagined Darcy's hand in Melanie's back pocket? It didn't necessarily mean anything. Maybe it had been a projection of my own cheek-palming desires. In any case, her email invigorated me. I gave Chad a call and let him know I was up for coming out. He told me to be at "The Injured Grizzly" at nine.

"So glad you decided to join us, buddy!" Chad shouted over the way-too-loud indie rock. He poured me a glass of beer from one of the three pitchers on the table.

"Yeah, it's nice to finally get to talk to you," Farah added. She was wearing a breast-spilling top and a skirt so short it was more like a thick belt. Despite the attire she seemed nice enough. "Chad has told me so many stories already."

"Nothing too bad I hope," I said, because that's what you're supposed to say.

"Not yet. So I hear you're an exterminator."

I sipped my beer. "That's right."

"That's so interesting!" She put her chin in her hands. "You must have seen some pretty nasty things. Got any horror stories?"

"Tell her about the hospital," Chad said.

"Oh no! A *hospital*? You're kidding."

I cleared my throat. "You know how everybody wants to 'go green' these days? I mean, take this place for example. Save the bears, animal cruelty, all that shit. A few months back, some hospital administrator has this genius idea to implement a composting plan for getting rid of food waste. They bring in these massive composting bins and plop them on a small patch of grass out back. Start putting all the leftover scraps from the cafeteria inside. Next thing you know, thousands, I'm talking *thousands* of rats are hanging around. Feasting. Screwing. Breeding. Sneaking inside through the air vents, making lab rats out of themselves. We found a whole pile of them dead near some boxes of insulin in one of the storage rooms."

"Oh my God. Did you get rid of them?"

"Hey," Chad said. "This is my *man* we're talking about."

"We think we did. It's hard to know for sure, especially with rats."

"Which hospital was it?"

I shrugged. "Sorry. I signed a confidentiality agreement."

"Jesus." Farah bit her nails.

"Who wants another round?" Chad asked.

I was about to offer to pay when a hand gripped my shoulder from behind. A gravelly voice said, "Excuse me?"

I spun around and looked directly into Darcy Sands' yellow eyeballs.

"I thought that was you. The Kill 'Em All guy, right?"

"Yeah, that's right. Do I . . . ?"

"You fumigated my place last week. Really fucked me up for a philosophy essay."

"Oh yeah. I remember. Sorry about that."

He stared into my face without blinking. I waited for him to speak but he didn't.

After a moment I said, "So. How's it going?"

"Hunky-dory, my friend! You don't mind if I call you *friend*, do you?"

Chad sat up straight. "What do you want, buddy?"

Darcy scratched the sparse whiskers on his chin. "I want to buy this man here a drink." He slapped me hard on the back.

I looked at Chad. He shrugged. Farah put her hand to her
chest in what I assumed was an attempt to hide her cleavage
from the greasy stranger hanging over our table.

I stood up. I was a good four or five inches taller than Darcy.
His matted hair smelled of gravy and hairspray.

"What's your poison?" he asked as we walked to the bar.

"Just a beer, thanks."

He sucked his teeth. "You sure? My man Viktor makes one
hell of a Bloody Paw Caesar."

"Beer's fine."

We sat down. Viktor Lozowsky, the owner, was shaking up
a martini behind the bar, his thick-rimmed glasses bouncing up
and down on his nose.

"Hey Vik!" Darcy shouted. "Can we get a beer down here?
Your cheapest brand, please." He turned to me. "I'm a firm
believer that someone's choice of drink says more about them
than anything else. You know what beer says? Boring."

"Listen, man," I said. "If you brought me over here to be
ridiculed, I'd just as soon go back to my friends."

"You're seeing Mel on Thursday."

"Huh?"

"*Huh?*" he said, imitating me, his pale tongue hanging out.
"You're meeting her here on Thursday."

"That's right. So what?"

We were interrupted by Viktor. He plunked a foamy pint in
front of me. "One boring beer for Mr. Excitement. Anything
else?"

"The usual for me," Darcy said.

"'The usual'?" I asked him. "What's that?"

He counted the ingredients off on his fingers: "Shot of
tequila. Shot of vodka. Shot of gin. Shot of rum. Fill the

rest of the glass with root beer and you've got an Adios Motherfucker."

"And what's that supposed to say about you?"

His yellow eyes seemed to flash. "No fucking fear."

Viktor returned and placed a soupy mixture in front of Darcy. "You puke, you mop."

Darcy took a sip and swallowed noisily. "*Sanguinis Christi*," he said. "Back to Mel. And you. And Thursday."

I sipped my beer and waited.

"So it's like this," he went on. "She's my best friend. I look out for her, make sure she doesn't get mixed up with assholes — especially assholes who refer to themselves as Mr. Exterminator. Or are you going by Mr. Excitement now?"

I didn't know what to say.

"Yeah." He raised his eyebrows. "You don't think I know her email password?" He leaned back and sipped his concoction. There was a whitehead on his neck that could have exploded at any moment.

I wanted to tell the dirtbag that it was Melanie who'd given me the name, but what good would it have done? I didn't need to tell him shit.

"What do you want from me?"

He chugged his drink and slammed the mug down onto the counter. "I want you guys to have a good time," he said, foam dripping from the sides of his mouth. "And if you hurt her, I'll fucking kill you."

It was the first time I'd been threatened with death. I won't lie — it scared the shit out of me. But I didn't want to give Darcy the satisfaction. I stonily downed the last of my beer. "Fair enough. We done?"

He turned to face the bar. "You betcha."

"What was *that* about?" Farah asked when I returned to the table. Chad looked up from his basket of wings.

"Just some asshole," I said. "You guys save some for me, or what?"

The following Monday, Bill and I were sent to an old textile warehouse on the west side. They were experiencing the second coming of a pharaoh ant problem that our competition, Eco-Zap, had fucked up royally. The thing about pharaoh ants is, if you don't eliminate every last one, the colony will split and multiply. Sprays don't cut it, either. You have to use insecticide baits, and you've got to put them *everywhere*.

I got to work right away while Bill sat on a pile of bricks with his thermos of coffee and a copy of *The Frayne Exchange*. "Listen to this," he said. "'Councillor proposes *Sweep the Streets* campaign in effort to reduce prostitution, STD infection.'"

POISON
SHY

I was down on my hands and knees, attempting to slide an ant trap into a crack in the wall. "Sounds like they're talking about small-scale genocide."

"We should be so lucky," he said. "Says here they want to feed and house the freaks. Offer them counselling paid for with *your* tax dollars. Jeez Louise."

It was a good half hour before Bill decided to join me. He farted as he squatted to remove the plastic cover on an electrical outlet. I turned to comment and got an eyeful. "You know, Bill, you would have made a good plumber."

He responded with another crackling gust.

"Christ, Bill."

"Sorry, kid — why don't you do us both a favour and get some more coffee? You've been working hard, and I've been shitting my pants all morning."

"Sure. You want anything else?"

He struggled to pluck the mini screwdriver out of his Swiss army knife. "No, just a coffee. Lotsa cream, lotsa sugar."

I hurried to fetch the coffees from a Tim Hortons across the road, and was almost run over by a minivan on the way back. I lingered outside the warehouse and caught my breath.

There was something in my back pocket. I reached inside and pulled out the crumpled photograph I'd taken from Melanie's apartment. She couldn't have been more than fifteen or sixteen in it. Drinking vodka. Screaming. Looking at it made me feel like a criminal.

Bill had done a decent amount of work while I was gone. He'd finished putting traps in the walls and was up on a ladder removing some of the ceiling tiles.

"Is it safe to enter?" I asked.

"All clear. But things could change after lunch."

We spent the rest of the morning stuffing the place with

ant traps. We left no floorboard unturned or wall crack unpoisoned. Bill offered to buy lunch, and brought back two ham and Swiss baguettes from Tim Hortons.

"The price of a sandwich, Jesus," he said.

We sat down cross-legged on a small patch of grass outside the building like a couple of kids at a picnic. Bill's legs cracked as he made himself comfortable. His round, red face smiled at me and then he dug in. He was unmarried and overweight, with IBS and a nose mutilated by too many years of hard Canadian rye. I thought he must be lonely. It struck me that I didn't know much about Bill. I knew he liked the Maple Leafs. I knew he owned a cottage up north that had been passed down through his family over generations, and that he stayed there when he wanted to do some deer or bear hunting. I knew he didn't like vegetables unless they were deep fried or sprinkled over nachos. For the most part he was nothing more than my jolly supervisor, as much a mystery to me as any middle-aged stranger I passed on the street. Who was I to assume Bill was lonely? He probably had things figured out far better than I did.

"Before I forget," he said, wiping his mouth with his sandwich wrapper. "I wasn't supposed to say anything, but I'd feel like an asshole if I didn't."

"Oh?" I thought he might be joking. He was almost always joking.

He took a deep breath. "Dick asked me to keep an eye on you."

Dick was our boss, the head honcho at Kill 'Em All. The guy who'd hired me on a whim. I kept quiet and fidgeted with my sandwich wrapper, tore it into smaller and smaller bits.

"He said he's worried you might be involved in some kind of funny business, calling in sick a lot lately and stuff. He thinks

49

your life outside the company might be interfering with your work. I told him not to worry. I said, Brandon's a good worker. A no-bullshit kind of guy."

"Thanks, Bill. I appreciate it." I held up my sandwich to him in salute.

"You got it."

We sat in silence for a moment, then Bill said, "Everything *is* okay with you, though, right? No problems at home? I don't mean to be a jerk but I gotta ask."

"No, everything's fine." I mustered a thin smile. It seemed to satisfy him.

"Great." He clapped his hands together and grunted as he wobbled to his feet. "Now, give me ten minutes to empty my guts and we can get back to work."

Bill wheezed on his way to the porta-potty. I tossed my half-eaten sandwich into a nearby garbage can and watched as a halo of flies claimed it for their own.

The days came and went. When I got home from work on Thursday, I checked myself out in the mirror. My skin was yellow-grey, almost translucent. I looked like a fucking zombie. What did I expect? I probably inhaled more poison in a single day than most people are exposed to in a year.

I got in the shower and scrubbed my whole body twice over. Shaved my face and coated it with aloe. Dug the dirt out from under my nails and trimmed my pubes with a stubby pair of Ninja Turtles scissors I'd had since childhood.

I lay down for a nap and dreamed I was digging a grave that kept refilling itself. I had to double my efforts if I wanted to make any progress with the ditch. At one point my shovel struck something hard. I jabbed at the thing, hoping to break through whatever it was. When I scraped the dirt away I saw that what I'd struck was a face — Melanie's — pulped and lacerated from my shovel thrusts. I woke with a ringing in my ears, my heart beating fast.

I nuked a frozen Salisbury steak and ate it slowly, choking it down.

After my meal I put on my best pair of jeans and a green and black argyle sweater, then sat down on my pullout and stared at the red glow of my alarm clock. 9:13.

I closed my eyes and counted to ten. Opened them. 9:13.

I poured myself a glass of red wine, some inexpensive merlot a client had sent to Kill 'Em All as a thank-you gift. Somehow I'd ended up with the bottle. I bounced my knee anxiously up and down and waited for the clock to change. The wine whirlpooled in the glass. How the hell was it still 9:13?

My hands were slimy with sweat. I stood up and wiped them on the ass pockets of my jeans. Looked at myself in the mirror.

"Relax, pussy," I said. "What's your problem? Chill . . . the fuck . . . out."

I wanted my reflection to open its mouth and speak, or psychically burn words of wisdom into my brain. Instead I noticed a nose hair curling sharply out of my left nostril.

I went to the bathroom and plucked the bad boy out. When I checked the time again it was 9:20. If I walked slowly to The Bloody Paw I'd arrive just before ten, with enough time to down a shot of liquid courage before Melanie showed up.

The night was breezy. The wind whispered through the trees like a scheming god. Discarded food wrappers cackled along the pavement. Cab drivers prowled the streets and hollered at girls in skirts too short for the weather and heels too high for the uneven sidewalk. A bus zoomed past as I stood waiting to cross the street. Its momentum almost pulled me onto the road.

As I neared the string of campus bars, someone behind me shouted, "Brandon Galloway eats dick!"

I spun around and saw Chad, his arm wrapped around Farah's gourd-like waist. The top four buttons on his shirt were undone, exposing a mass of wiry chest hair. Farah smelled as though she'd just taken a bath in Chanel No. 5.

Chad cocked his head at me. "Hot date?" He turned to Farah. "What'd I tell you? The guy's a Casanova."

"I'm meeting Melanie, actually."

Chad lowered his eyebrows and pursed his lips. He looked like an ape. "Melanie . . ."

"The redhead."

"Oh! Right on. We're hitting up Shock for martinis." He leaned toward me and mock-whispered, "I'm gonna get her *smashed!*"

Farah whacked him playfully on the shoulder.

"All right, we better get going," Chad said. "I want to make sure we get the loveseat by the fireplace."

They started down the street, Chad's right hand clinging firmly to Farah's backside. As I waited to cross the road, Chad shouted, "Hey Brandon! Don't forget to equip your little soldier before you send him into battle! You can never be too careful!" He threw back his head and laughed.

I zigzagged through a gathering of future lung cancer patients outside The Bloody Paw and found a seat at the bar. Melanie wasn't there. Viktor Lozowsky stood behind the beer taps, setting shots on fire. When he finished, he handed the flaming glasses to a white girl with dreadlocks and her purple-haired boyfriend. They blew out their drinks and gulped them down in unison. The boyfriend let out a whoop and wiped his eyes, while the girl thumped her chest with a toddler-sized fist.

"What can I get you?"

Lozowsky seemed to be looking just to the right of my face. The ceiling lights reflected off his waxy bald head. I wasn't sure he was speaking to me.

"You deaf or something, slim?"

"Sorry, I . . . I'll wait to order if that's okay. I'm meeting someone."

He slung a greasy towel over his shoulder. "I remember you. The boring beer guy."

I tried to laugh but it came out in a sneeze.

"You mind if I ask who you're meeting? I get a lot of regulars in here."

I looked at the nest of crumpled twenties bursting from his pouch. "Her name's Melanie."

"Melanie Blaxley? Red hair?" He snickered. "She was just here. I think she went to the bathroom. Hopefully she's not barfing all over the hand dryer. It was expensive to replace last time."

A loud cat-call came from behind me. I turned and there was Melanie, strutting out of the bathroom in yellow short shorts and a black baby-tee. It had an image of a giraffe with the words DEEP THROAT written along its neck in letter-shaped spots. On her feet she wore a pair of pink pumps, small enough for a doll. She stuck up her middle finger at the guy who'd whistled — a Che Guevara wannabe in a beret — and continued in my direction, hips swaying. Her unsupported breasts vibrated with each step.

"You're late, prick. And you better close your mouth or you're going to drool all over your zipper."

"Sorry, I — Aren't you cold?"

"Weather doesn't scare me." I caught a whiff of her perfume (raspberries) and her armpits (sweet chili).

"Ready to order?" Lozowsky asked.

I had to think for a moment. "Yeah, I'll have . . . Let's see. I'll have a rum and Coke."

"Psshh." Melanie shook her head.

"What?"

She ignored me and turned to Viktor. "Give me the usual. In a frosted mug this time."

"The usual?" I asked her. "What's that?"

"It's this awesome drink called an Adios Motherfucker. Whole bunch of shit mixed into root beer. I forget the ingredients but it fucks you good and hard. I saw this clip on YouTube where these dudes chug them, then barf into one of those plastic pumpkins kids use for trick-or-treating. They mix all their pukes together with a ladle and dump it on some passed-out chick like a barf bukkake. It's fucking hilarious! This drink is the shiz, niggz."

I quickly scanned the bar. No black people anywhere, thank God.

Lozowsky came over with the drinks. "You two on separate tabs?"

"Nah! Bug Man here's gonna buy all my drinks tonight. We're on a date." She slapped and squeezed my thigh.

Her touch set off a series of loin-centred explosions that forced me to adjust myself. I took out my wallet and robotically tossed bill after bill onto the counter like a bank clerk.

"Whoa, Money Man!" Melanie said. Lozowsky stuffed the bills into his pouch. "Well, this should cover you for about a week. Cheers!" Then he was gone.

Melanie picked up her mug with both hands and took a

big gulp. Threads of amber liquid ran down the sides of her mouth and dripped onto her bare knees. "Shit, that's harsh!" She wiped the booze off her knees with her palm, then brought her hand to her face and licked it.

"That's your roommate's drink of choice too, isn't it?"

"Darcy's? How would you know that?"

"I saw him order one."

"He stole it from me. How's your rum and Coke, sailor?"

"It's good."

"Fuck that. Get something more exciting next round. This place is, like, *known* for its cool drinks. The Bloody Paw Caesar's got mashed-up jalapeños in it. Ice cream vodka's not bad, but it gives me brain freeze. The best is the champagne whisky bomb, aside from the Adios Motherfucker, of course."

I sipped my drink. It actually wasn't very good. I didn't know why I'd said that. "How long have you known Darcy, anyway?"

"Since first year. He lived down the hall from me in rez. Helped me write my essays a bunch of times. If it weren't for him I probably would have flunked out. Why?"

"Just figured you must be pretty good friends to decide to be roommates."

"Is someone jealous?"

"Not at all, I just —"

"But yeah, he's a cool guy. Weird, but cool. But who *isn't* weird, you know?"

"Are you weird?"

"Me?" She leaned in close. Licked her lips and crossed her eyes. "I'm fucking insane!"

We had a few drinks at the bar, then moved to a two-person booth in the corner. On the wall above our table was a giant portrait of a dead polar bear, half-buried in a glacier, the landscape a sheet of nothingness.

Every now and then Lozowsky would approach, swinging dish rags like they were nunchucks, and take our orders with his eyes closed and his hands in his pockets.

"You kids should feel honoured," he told us while delivering our fourth round of champagne whisky bombs. "I don't usually wait tables. I expect a big tip."

"Do you believe that guy?" I said after he'd gone.

"What do you mean?"

"I don't know, he seems . . . I don't know."

"Viktor's the best."

"'You kids should feel honoured.' *Kids*? Give me a break."

"Who cares?"

"Okay, you're right. I'm sorry."

"You get worked up when you drink, don't you?"

"Not usually."

"It's okay." She giggled. "It's kind of hot."

"Really?"

"Fuck yeah."

I didn't know what to say, so I kept drinking.

"I don't normally go on dates, you know," she said. "Like, date dates."

"No?"

"Nope. When I came to university, my policy was no relationships, just fun."

"Is that why you wear that shirt?"

"No. I wear this shirt because it was a gift. From Viktor, actually."

"I don't understand."

"I went out with him once, a few months ago. It wasn't a date like this. Just a one-time thing." She stared into the arctic portrait. "Good times."

I didn't say anything for a while. She went on at length about the people she'd been out with the past two years: a guitarist in a punk band, one of her TAs, a hockey player with three testicles, a married man from Toronto who'd drive out to Frayne every second weekend. Even a Goth chick from her art history class.

"One thing I learned: I do *not* like the taste of pussy."

As she went on and on, I took a look around at the bar's dwindling clientele. Turnip Head and his Rastafarian princess were still hanging around, along with a table of political science nerds sporting buttons that read *Pesticides Kill*.

I looked over at the bar, which had been empty only moments ago, and saw Darcy Sands sitting alone, staring at us, a sweating Molson in his hand.

My knees bashed the underside of the table.

"Nervous twitch much?" Melanie said.

I nodded toward the bar. "I think your friend's here to see you."

She spun her head. "Hey homo! Quit staring."

Darcy stood up and staggered to our booth. "I'm surprised — you're still here." He thunked his beer on the table, missing my hand by inches. "Shouldn't you be face deep in each other's crotches by now?"

"You smell like ass," Melanie said.

He scratched his chin whiskers with dirt-blackened fingernails. "I'm taking you home, Mel."

"No."

"Why not?"

"Because you're not, that's why."

Darcy swayed and almost fell over. "Fine, I get it. I get it. Tell me. Are you gonna let him fuck you in the ass?"

I stood up. "All right, that's enough."

"That's enough what?" He looked up into my face. His eyes were slits.

"Can you mind your own business?"

"Listen, you twat." He jerked forward and grabbed the collar of my shirt. Pulled something out of his pocket and pressed it against my throat.

"Darcy!" Melanie yelled, like she was scolding him.

I grabbed his wrist and dragged his hand away. There was a small penknife in his hand.

He swung at me with the beer bottle in his other hand. It flew out of his grip and smashed against the wall.

I was frozen with shock. The bar went quiet.

"Take that bullshit outside, you hear me?" Lozowsky shouted.

"It's Darcy," Melanie said. "He's being a dick."

"All right d-bag, that's enough." Lozowsky marched out from behind the bar and charged at him.

"I wasn't — hey! I wasn't doing . . . Let go of me, you tree-hugging warlock! I'm gonna sue your ass! Then what will you do, huh? Go back to drinking piss in some gutter in Warsaw?"

Darcy continued to hurl insults as Lozowsky threw him out onto the street.

"Holy shit," I said. "What's his problem?"

Melanie shrugged. "He's just drunk, that's all. No big deal."

"He pull that sort of thing all the time?"

"I guess. So, you got any booze at your place?"

"I think so. Why?"

"Because that's where we're going, dummy."

She adjusted her breasts and headed for the door. I followed her, admiring the trail of creases the vinyl seats had left on the backs of her thighs.

We passed a lineup of taxis parked outside.

"Do we need a cab?" Melanie asked.

"We can walk."

She stepped on a crack in the sidewalk and stumbled. I caught her wrist and kept her from falling.

"Damn heels." She plucked them off and continued walking in bare feet.

"You okay like that?"

"Why wouldn't I be?"

"I don't know. You could step on a rusty nail or a hypodermic needle."

She laughed. "A hypodermic needle? You're such a loser."

We walked along Dormant Street, the cobwebbed streetlamps lighting our way in glimmering orange patches. Splattered on the curb, beside the last taxi at the end of the block, was a soupy puddle of beige vomit.

"Gross," Melanie said as she jumped to avoid it.

I looked back over my shoulder. It was hard to see through the tinted glass, but I thought I could make out a figure in the taxi's back seat, staring at us from somewhere behind my warped reflection.

If I am in a skull-cracking car accident and suffer amnesia, or if I develop Alzheimer's, or even if I die and there's no heaven, I will always remember that first night with Melanie Blaxley.

We got to my place just after two. I offered her a glass of wine from the bottle I'd opened earlier, but she refused.

"This place smells like candy canes. Where's your bathroom?"

I pointed to the wide-open door, right beside where she was standing, through which my toilet and sink were both visible. She went inside and slammed the door hard. I thought about the prostitute who'd puked in there just last week. It felt like eons ago.

The toilet flushed, then flushed again. I heard the scrape of my plastic garbage can across the tiles. The tap. The squeak of my medicine cabinet. Another flush.

"Everything okay in there?"

"Coming!"

The reality of the situation hit me: I was going to get laid. My saliva turned hot. I sat down. The door swung open.

"Sorry about that." She skipped over and sat next to me on the couch. Crossed her legs. "Don't mind the pad in your garbage can. I'm on my rag."

"Oh."

She lunged forward and planted her lips on my cheek. "How old are you?"

"Twenty-nine."

"Really? You seem younger."

"Everyone tells me that."

"I would have said twenty-three. At the oldest."

"Nope."

"Got any ID there, buddy?"

I tried to laugh.

She put her hand on my leg. "Why are you holding your hands like that? Don't tell me you're *praying*. Are you a virgin?"

"No, no. And I'm not praying."

"Then why don't you touch my tits?"

"Huh?"

"Come on." She ran her fingernail along the seam of my jeans. "You're so stiff. Are you sure you're not a virgin? You can admit it. I'm still gonna let you fuck me."

"I thought you said you're on your period."

"Yeah, so?"

"I . . ."

She threw her head back and laughed. "I've never fucked anyone so nice before." She pulled off her T-shirt in one smooth motion. Her pale, small-nippled breasts were dusted with freckles. "Come on, let's get you hard."

She got down onto her knees and scraped her nails up my legs to my zipper. I could feel my heartbeat in my neck.

A glistening dribble of saliva hung on her bottom lip. "What are you going to do to me, Brandon?"

It was the first time I'd heard her say my name. I looked up at my ceiling and mouthed a thank-you at the browned water stain in the corner.

But then something happened. I looked down at the orange mane bobbing between my legs, and the face that turned up to meet my gaze wasn't sprightly and freckled, not Melanie's face at all, but the smirking, wrinkled mug of Suzie the prostitute.

"Jesus!"

"What? What's wrong?" She was Melanie once again, startled and annoyed.

"I . . . I don't . . ."

"Give me a fucking break." She stood up and stomped into the kitchen, the crease of her shorts wedged into her ass crack. She poured herself a mug of water from the tap and drank it with her back to me.

"Melanie, I'm sorry. I think I had too much to drink."

She dropped the mug into the sink; it crashed against my unwashed plates. "So did I!"

I stared into my lap and fingered the crotch button on my boxer shorts.

"Where's that wine?" She opened the fridge, moved some things around, closed it. Stood on her toes and reached up to look through my cupboards, her naked breasts stretching out and flattening against her chest.

"Listen," I said. "If you want to leave, I'll understand. I'm really sorry about this."

She found the wine on the counter next to the toaster oven and took a swig straight from the bottle. "And go back home to Darcy? No fucking way. I'm staying here whether you like it or not. If your dick decides to wake up, let me know. I'm going to bed."

I scrambled off the couch and converted it to bed mode. Melanie stood behind me like a dominatrix, holding the bottle of wine by its neck. It swayed between her legs like a pendulum. I got the feeling she wasn't afraid to use it on me if necessary.

Once the bed was made, she shoved me aside and crawled under the sheets. She was out within seconds. I sat on the edge of the mattress and watched her sleep with the resigned composure of a born loser. Had I really been so naïve as to expect, or even hope for, a happy ending to the night?

I went for a pee, and returned to find Melanie sprawled out diagonally across the mattress, snoring like a moose on her drool-dampened pillow. I eased myself down onto the very edge, my shoulder pressed against the cold metal bar of the bed frame. I had no sheets, no room to move around and get comfortable.

After twenty restless minutes of shivering, I turned onto my stomach and blasted the night's disappointment into the hollow darkness of my apartment with one long, deflating fart. Sleep came a bit easier after that.

I dreamed I was wrapped in a cocoon sealed with a zipper. It was full of water, but somehow I was able to breathe. I was warm and comfortable, but I couldn't shake the feeling that something wasn't right. Before long the water started to boil. I reached up to open the zipper but couldn't find the tag. The casing was sealed from the outside. My flesh started to blister. I tried to scream but no sound came out of my mouth.

In an instant the water evaporated. Something had landed on top of the cocoon, puncturing it with its weight. A kind of peace flowed through me. I had goosebumps. My crotch seemed to glow.

The zipper tore open and I was slurped back into waking life, though what I saw when I opened my eyes was more frightening than any dream.

Melanie sat on top of me, fully naked, eyes frosted like her vision had turned inward. Her face and body were covered with streaks and handprints of her own menstrual blood. She writhed on top of me like a serpent. Ran her blood-smeared hands through her hair, across her nipples, along my chest, marking me.

"What —"

She grasped at me and put me inside her. She was warm, extremely wet. I tried to look into her face but all I saw was a dark mask. She leaned forward, dug her nails into my scalp, held me down.

The realization that I wasn't wearing a condom hit me like a dart. I tried to pull myself out from under her but she slapped me hard across the face. Grunted. One of her nails broke off against my skull. She cried out and leaned backward, breasts to the sky, arms and shoulders loose. Her thighs squeezed my hips with every contraction.

I lay there, panting and swollen. There was blood every-where. I could smell it.

"Melanie . . ."

She didn't move. She was frozen, like a human spider crab, in the most uncomfortable position I'd ever seen. If it weren't for the subtle rising and falling of her abdomen, I'd have thought her neck had snapped and she was dead.

"Melanie, you okay?"

Finally she collapsed onto the mattress. "Damn. I needed that."

"So you *are* alive."

"You too." She turned and bent over the side of the bed in search of her underwear, her goosepimpled ass in my face. It, too, was smeared with blood.

"What just happened?"

She stood and slid her panties up her thighs. "Um, I just fucked you."

"I mean, what's with the . . . I've never . . ."

She patted me on the cheek. "I'm female. I bleed once a month. It's a little something called biology."

"Yeah, but —"

"Shove over, stud. I'm going back to sleep."

"Like *that*?"

"I'm tired, okay? Send me your laundry bill. Now, shove over!"

I went to the bathroom to rinse myself off while she bur-rowed under the covers. Squinting into the mirror, I saw the face of a confused young man with a bloody handprint on his cheek. I coughed and spat into the sink. Told myself this was it. Now that I'd slept with her I could go back to my normal life, killing bugs in strangers' homes and drinking my face off with Chad. I could even get used to Farah being around. Maybe the three of us could go on a road trip to Montreal and see what Patricia was up to.

I wiped my chest and hands with a wet towel and went back to the pull-out. Melanie was asleep again, or pretending to be. She looked like a murder victim, something out of a movie.

I woke the next morning in a tangle of bloodstained sheets. Melanie was no longer beside me. I checked the clock: just after eight. I had to be at work in less than an hour.

"Hello?" I said, a stranger in my own home. "Anyone here?"

The plumbing clicked in the walls.

"Melanie?"

Nothing.

I sat upright. My vision blurred into a kaleidoscopic swirl of purple and beige. My mouth was dry as cement mix. I could smell the vinegary scent of my armpits despite the stench of dried blood. I needed a hot shower, a large glass of water, and possibly an exorcist.

When my vision returned I noticed a torn piece of paper tacked to the back of my front door. Something was scribbled on it in pink highlighter. I wobbled over and read it:

> *Had to run to work*
> *Don't choke on your breakfast and die*
> *Mel   444-6187*

I crumpled the note and shot it at my garbage can as though it were a miniature basketball. It bounced off the edge and fell to the floor.

"Fuck it," I muttered.

After gulping a few litres of water straight from my kitchen tap and sterilizing myself in a scalding hot shower, I began to feel human again. I burned some frozen waffles, covered them in syrup, and devoured them in seconds.

My uniform was buried in a pile of dirty laundry in the closet. I threw it on in a hurry and nearly fell down my front steps on my way out. Two teenaged boys with white-blond hair sat on the bench outside the laundromat with folders in their laps and brochures in their chest pockets.

"Excuse me, sir," one of them called as I rushed past. "Are you interested in hearing about the Church of Jesus Christ of Latter-Day Saints?"

"Maybe," I said, quickening my pace. "But I don't think He'd be interested in hearing about me."

I stumbled into work right on time, only to have Dick inform me I'd been assigned another bedbug job across town. Bill had taken the van and was already on site. Dick dropped an oily bus token in my hand and glared at me without a word as I backed out of the office.

The bus was full of strangers who judged me from behind their stolid commuters' masks. Tweens with mp3 players, grannies with drug store paperbacks, basement dwellers scouring want ads. I sat next to an obscenely thin woman in a fur coat who smelled like coffee. Her bony legs, all nylons and varicose veins, hung over the seat like sausage links. She held a transfer in front of her, pinched between thumb and forefinger, as though she was reading the world's smallest newspaper.

It took me a moment to realize it was my landlady, Bette. It would be awkward to talk to her outside the monthly ritual of dropping my rent in her mailbox, so I kept quiet and checked under my seat for something to read. I found a page torn from the sports section of the *Toronto Sun*, a dusty shoeprint stamped across the logo for the Toronto Maple Leafs. "Buds Drop Sixth in a Row." I started to read about how the referees were to blame for the loss when Bette placed her wrinkled hand on my knee.

"Brandon. I thought that was you."

"Oh, hello, Bette. Since when do you take Frayne transit?"

"Since my Dodge broke down. A piece of advice: never buy an American car. Japanese is the way to go."

"I'll keep that in mind for when I'm in the market."

The bus went over a pothole and Bette fell into my lap. As I helped her settle back into her seat, the photograph I'd taken from Melanie's apartment fell out of my pocket and onto the floor. Bette reached down and picked it up before I could get to it.

"Isn't she a pretty one! Girlfriend?" She held the photo two inches in front of her face.

"Yes. Well, no. Well, kind of. She's —"

POISON
SHY

"A little young for the likes of you."

"It's an old picture."

She attempted to fix the creases in the photo by folding them back against themselves. "Reminds me of me when I was young."

The hair on the back of my neck prickled. "Oh yeah?"

"Yessir. I had dark hair, mind you. And no freckles. And I've worn glasses all my life. But other than that, she's my spitting image!" She handed the photo back to me and looked at the name sewn onto my uniform. "Why does your uniform have the name Dennis on it?"

"When they hired me they gave me a spare and never bothered to get it changed."

"I see. I guess you can pretend to be someone else while you're zapping bugs. That's kind of fun."

"I've never tried that, but you know what? It sounds like a good idea." I stuffed the photograph back into my pocket and stood up. "Well, this is my stop."

"What a coinkidink. Mine too. I've got to collect some rent from a deadbeat tenant who's always late with his payments. Would you mind helping me up?"

She grabbed my forearm and pulled herself out of her seat. She was barely five feet tall. When she reached up to ding the bell she nearly toppled over. I noticed an alligator-skin flask sticking out the pocket of her fur coat as I followed her to the exit door.

When I stepped off the bus behind her, a gust of wind blew some grit into my eye. I dug my knuckle into my socket, and when I opened my eyes again, I saw a bald Bette chasing her hair down the street, her fur coat flopping heavily behind her like the dead animal it was. I had no idea she wore a wig.

I caught up to the tumbling coif, plucked it off the sidewalk, and slapped it against my thigh. A cloud of dust exploded from it. Pebbles fell to the sidewalk. I sneezed.

"Thank you very much," Bette said, catching her breath. She took an inhaler out of her pocket and puffed on it. Her pockmarked scalp was coated with a cobwebby fuzz.

I handed her the wig, but she didn't put it on right away. Instead, she removed the flask from her pocket and offered me a drink.

"No thanks," I said.

She unscrewed the cap, took a swig. "Cancer," she said, and shrugged.

"Bette, I had no idea. I'm sorry."

She waved a hand at me as if to dismiss it. "Bad things happen to everyone."

I bit my lip as she walked away. There really was something poisonous about this town, where even the wealthy were doomed. Down the block I saw the Kill 'Em All van parked outside a tenement. Bill was leaning against the hatch eating a doughnut.

"'Bout time," he said as I approached. There was a smear of raspberry jelly on the upper of his chins.

"Sorry."

He opened the passenger door and took out a box of doughnuts. "Want one? They're fresh as shit."

By the time our client had cleared out of the apartment, we'd eaten the whole box. And then we fumigated the hell out of the place. As we were loading up the van to leave, Melanie's picture fell out of my pocket again.

"What do we have here?" Bill said. He bent to pick it up.

"It's nothing."

He stared intensely at the photograph for a moment, then flicked the corner and nodded. "The doughnut shop."

"Huh?"

He spat onto the curb, a long sugary rope of pink goo. "Darryl's Doughnuts. This chick works there. Bought the dozen off her this morning."

"Really."

"Why? Did you bang her last night or something?"

"What?"

"Hey, I'm just asking. You have a picture of her, for Chrissakes."

"Give me that," I said, and snatched the photo out of his hands.

"Jeez, Brandon, relax. She's not your sister, is she? Shit, I'm sorry. I gotta learn to shut my damn trap once in a while."

"No, Bill. It's fine. I'm sorry. Bad day, that's all. Come on, I'll buy lunch. You down for Chinese?"

I decided, over my box of chow mein, to burn the stolen photograph of Melanie as soon as I got home, and never to set foot in Darryl's Doughnuts again. Then I read my fortune cookie:

Be mischievous and you will never be alone.

The universe was fucking with me. I said goodbye to Bill and felt my demons tug my bones in the direction of Melanie's work.

I saw her through the window from the parking lot out front. She sat behind the counter on a stool in a pink and green striped apron that was covered in patches of icing sugar. Her hair, bunched up in a hairnet, stuck out like a wasp's nest through the hole atop her pink visor. The shop was empty. She leafed through the pages of some celebrity gossip magazine and yawned.

Was this the same girl who'd ravaged me the night before? Who'd initiated me into a world of blood-soaked sexual aerobics? Who'd turned me into a mindless follower of fortune cookie proverbs?

She looked up from her magazine and saw me. Stood up and smoothed her apron against her body. Waved me in.

"Nice uniform," she said as I stepped inside. "You look like the creepy janitor at my old high school who used to write me secret love poems."

"Thanks for the compliment. You look like one of Santa's elves."

"I think you mean the Easter Bunny's personal slave." She slid her fingertips along the brim of her visor. "How'd you find out where I work, stalker?"

"I didn't. I always come here."

"Well, I've worked here for almost a year and I've never seen you."

"I guess that's a fluke."

"Or you're lying. But that's okay. I like it when guys come after me."

Is that what I was doing? I took a seat and asked for a decaf.

"You mean you're going to force me to do my job? That's cruel. Didn't I rock your cock last night? You should be nicer to me."

When she turned around to pour my coffee, I noticed she was still wearing the yellow shorts, pink pumps, and giraffe T-shirt she'd worn on our date.

"Didn't you stop at home before coming to work?" I asked.

"Didn't have time."

"You're telling me you came straight here from my place?"

She clip-clopped over with a saucer and coffee cup in hand and placed them on my table. I noticed the broken nail on her right index finger. "Relax, freak. I had a shower before I left but you were still asleep. Cream and sugar?"

"Just cream."

She pulled two creamers from the pouch on her apron and dropped them in my lap. "Better drink it fast. Darcy's on his way and I can't be held responsible for any violent outbursts."

"What are you talking about?"

She went back to her stool and picked up the magazine. "He called here just after my shift started. Wanted to know where I'd spent the night. I don't think he remembers anything from the bar." She casually flipped through some pages. "Anyway, he's never happy when I don't come home."

What did *that* mean?

I wanted to ask: Isn't he just a roommate? What kind of roommate waits up? Are you trying to make me paranoid? Are you saying I'm in danger?

I should have told her to stay out of my life, that I didn't play stupid games and that she and her fucked-up roommate could go straight to hell.

But I didn't. I couldn't. Because as I was fantasizing about splashing my tepid coffee in her face and storming out of there, the door jingled open and Darcy walked in.

"My professor is a fascist," he said as he took a seat at the doughnut bar. "He sent me an email this morning *informing* me that if I miss any more lectures I'll be *forced to accept* a ten percent penalty on my mid-term paper. Is that not the stankest pile of bull? What does my attendance have to do with the papers I write? I've based my whole academic career on skipping class and writing killer fucking essays. Class is for retards and ass-lickers. I may have to go to the department head about this."

He took a pair of bent cigarettes out of his pocket, placed one behind his ear, and stood the other on the counter facing up.

"Two smokes?" Melanie said, lip curling. "That's it?"

"I'm fucking broke, all right? Give me a break. Know what I ate for breakfast this morning? Cornflakes and water. And that was *after* puking. It tasted like bile. *And* there was a dead earwig in my bowl. Take what you get. Speaking of which, give me anything that's not stale."

Melanie stuck the cigarette between her lips and served Darcy a sticky cruller. He took a bite and turned to me.

"Afternoon, pops," he said, then did a double-take. *"You?"* He turned to Melanie. "What's *he* doing here?" Back to me. "She steal your wallet?"

I sipped my coffee. It was cold.

Melanie nudged Darcy's shoulder. "Give me a light."

Darcy took a soggy pack of matches out of his pocket and handed them over. There was just one match left in the pack, hanging off the end like a broken limb. Melanie folded it over and struck it against the black strip with one hand. She waited for Darcy to put his cigarette in his mouth and lit his first, then her own.

I stood up. The metal legs of my chair squealed along the floor. "I'm gonna get going."

"What's the matter?" Darcy said. "You don't want to hang out? Come on. I want to hear bug stories. Ever kill a human by mistake? Some neglected baby left in its crib? What's the lifespan of your average centipede? You know — the brownish ones you see in basements that make girls scream. Are you a snooper? A panty sniffer? Come on, Bug Man. What's the worst thing you've ever seen?"

"I'll see you around, Melanie," I said.

"Hang on," she said as I made my way to the door. She was trying not to laugh. "Are you really leaving?"

I shrugged then nodded.

"Okay, well, call me." She took a big pull on her cigarette and exhaled a vaporous cone in the direction of the ceiling.

"Or don't," Darcy added.

I left. Stuffed my hands in the lint-lined pockets of my uniform and walked slump-shouldered through Darryl's Doughnuts' parking lot, the wind echoing. An alarm went off behind me and my heart almost exploded. I turned around; Melanie and Darcy had set off the smoke detector with their cigarettes. Melanie crawled up onto the counter then onto Darcy's shoulders. Her shorts rode up her ass. Darcy gripped her kneecaps and held her steady. She swatted at the smoke alarm with a rag and accidentally kicked over a stack of Styrofoam cups. The alarm finally stopped. The two of them laughed like maniacs.

I walked home in the rain and fog. Stopped at the liquor store and picked up a case of beer called *La Fin du Monde* — a brand to reflect my mood. At the corner of my street I slipped on a flattened juice box and fell. Bashed up my elbows trying to keep the beer from smashing. Inside, I picked Melanie's note out of my garbage and put it in my sock drawer. Peeled the bloody sheets off my bed, stuffed them in a duffel bag and threw it across the room. Masturbated to the thought of tying her down and fucking her on the doughnut counter, then indulged in a deep, manly cry under the comfortless spray of a cold shower.

That night was Halloween. I went downstairs to the laundromat to wash the blood out of my bedsheets. The place was full of costumed students with baskets full of salty, yellowed underwear. They all seemed to know each other, like they'd planned some kind of All Hallows' Eve laundry social. I could still hear them laughing and cracking beers after I'd gone back upstairs. It took a fair amount of restraint not to throw myself out the window when they launched into an a capella version of "Monster Mash."

Fortunately they left after that — and that's when I started drinking.

While children roamed the streets begging candy from strangers, I sat flipping channels like a misanthropic shut-in. Sipped my beers with mechanical stillness, eyes glued to a reality show in which a band of white-trash strippers competed for the chance to date an over-the-hill rock star. I couldn't get enough. They were showing the whole season in a marathon session. I only left my spot on the couch three times: twice to pee, once to get my sheets out of the dryer. The stains had smudged and turned brown, but I didn't care. I didn't plan on seeing Melanie ever again. All I wanted to do was sit on my ass and drink until the sun came up. I kept the twelve-pack on the floor in front of me and used it as an ottoman. Each beer I cracked was warmer than its predecessor. The malty liquid sloshed in my belly whenever I scratched an itch or rubbed my eye.

I started to get drowsy. I fell asleep for a split second, then jerked awake to a parade of water-balloon breasts in stars-and-stripes bikinis. Outside, teenagers exploded pumpkins with cherry bombs, then ran away screaming.

I tortured myself with mental games: if they cut to commercial before the clock changes I'm going to die in my sleep. If I hear another pumpkin explosion in the next thirty seconds,

POISON
SHY

a murderer is going to break into my apartment and slash my throat. If someone — anyone — presses my buzzer, even if it's just a prank, the world will end.

I fell asleep to these horrors. I can't say how long I was out, but I woke up to a spinning room. I took off my shirt and laid down on the cold tiles of my bathroom floor, the toilet bowl safely within puking distance. My TV was still on in the other room. The network was playing classical music over a blank screen while it waited for its morning programming.

Eventually I felt well enough to crawl to the couch, but just as I'd wrapped myself in a blanket and settled into the fetal position, my buzzer sounded.

I froze, then swallowed a mouthful of spicy vomit. I braced myself for an earthquake, for the sidewalk to split, for eruptions of lava and swarms of giant insects to sweep in and devour all of humankind.

But nothing happened. The world was intact — of course it was. What was happening to me? Was I becoming my mother? I tiptoed to the window and peeped through the curtains. There were no pranksters running down the street, no cars peeling away. The one place I couldn't see was directly in front of the door. Was someone still waiting? A murderer? A *ghost*? I felt like a lunatic out of an Edgar Allan Poe story. Years of horror novels and zombie games had infected my brain.

I decided to go downstairs to check things out. I went to my closet and got the old T-ball bat I still had from when I was a kid. It was only about forty inches long, but it was painted blood red and had a killer nickname carved into the barrel: *Red Hot.* My own personal second amendment.

I held it in one hand like a club and slowly made my way down the stairs. I didn't expect to find anyone, but I was prepared to swing.

The door had no windows, no peephole. My plan was to turn the lock and pull it open with as close to a single motion as I could manage, then have a good chuckle at the expense of my own ridiculous paranoia.

I wiped my sweaty palm on my pants, gripped Red Hot, and turned the lock.

Melanie lay slumped on the concrete steps in a kitty-cat costume.

There was a puddle of bubblegum-pink vomit between her legs. She wore a low-cut ballet top and a see-through pair of black tights. A cat-ear headband hung around her neck like a collar. She looked up at me with squinty, mascara-caked eyes and mumbled something about a fight with Darcy and getting ditched. She said Darcy called her a dirty slut and splashed beer in her face. Stole her key and took off in a cab with some other friends. Told her to sleep at a bus station, where she belonged. She said she came here because she knew the way and didn't know where else to go. Her voice was as hoarse as a goblin's. I couldn't tell if she'd been crying or if she was just smashed.

I lifted her by the armpits and was surprised at how light she was, as though her bones were made of Styrofoam. She smelled strongly of sweet and spicy female body odour. I picked a dried leaf out of her hair as I followed her up the stairs, her pipecleaner cat's tail brushing my nose. Her black panties were visible through her stockings. I figured it was part of the outfit. Naughty pussycat: the most cliché party girl Halloween costume ever. I couldn't imagine her dressing up as anything else.

I sat her on my couch and brought her a glass of tap water. She gulped it down like a thirsty toddler, hiccupping twice. I brought her a blanket. Offered her something to eat. She shook her head and curled up with her fists under her chin, feet crossed at the ankles, painted-on whiskers smudged. She looked like a sad painting.

I sunk into my easy chair and watched her sleep, her nasal vibrations lulling me into a stupor, then drifted off myself.

The next morning I decided to make bacon and eggs. I heard her moan on her way to the bathroom. She peed with the door open and didn't flush, then shuffled into the kitchen looking haggard.

"Smells yummy." She stuck her hand down the back of her tights and adjusted her panties. "Do I get any?"

I drained grease into the sink. "I made it for you. Toast?"

She shrugged. "Can you make me a bacon and egg sandwich?"

"If that's what you want."

She helped herself to a mug of coffee and took a seat at the table. "Sorry about crashing. I don't even really know what happened."

"You said Darcy ditched you. Told you to sleep on the street."

"Yeah, I don't know. We fight a lot. It'll blow over." She yawned and sipped her coffee. "Do you work today?"

I slammed the still-soft slices of bread back into my piece-of-shit toaster. "You said he stole your key."

She laughed. "Yeah."

I felt my face burning. "Darcy seems like a real asshole."

"He's not that bad. He's got a temper, that's all. He puts up with a lot of my shit, too. I can dish it out just as bad as he can." She smiled as if reminiscing.

"Why do you always defend him?" I picked some bacon slices out of the frying pan with my fingers and slapped them on her toast. "The guy acts like he's your pimp or something and you just take it."

"He's my friend."

"He treats you like shit." I flipped the egg onto her sandwich and the yoke exploded; yellow goo speckled my countertop. "What's the deal with you guys? You say you're just room-mates but I get the feeling he's fucking you. And fucking *with* you."

She didn't respond. She just sat and looked at me.

I waited for my hands to stop shaking, then placed her sandwich on the table in front of her. "I'm sorry, okay? I didn't mean to get so worked up. But *God*. I just can't believe —"

"Fuck me."

"What?"

She stood up. "Fuck me. Right now."

I leaned in to kiss her. She grabbed the back of my neck and shoved her tongue in my mouth. We wobbled and crashed

POISON
SHY

around the kitchen as we shook off our clothes with frantic, jerky limbs. I spun her around and pressed her against the fridge. Pulled down her tights. Unzipped my fly and stuck myself inside her. She arched her back and took me in deeper. I leaned forward and pressed her against the fridge, turned her head to the side, and stuck my fingers in her mouth. She looked back at me. "Uunnghh." Ice cubes rattled with every thrust.

When it was over we collapsed together on the cold kitchen floor, our chests rising and falling in reverse unison. Melanie was the first to get up. She ran a hand through her messy hair, pulled up her pants, and sat back down at the table. Started eating her sandwich like it was a lazy Sunday morning. "Mmm," she said.

I stood up and poured some coffee. "I better get dressed."

"What are you doing later?" she asked with her mouth full.

Were Melanie Blaxley and I ever a couple? I can't say for sure. There were times I thought we were; then she'd do things to suggest otherwise, like introduce me as her "buddy," give her phone number to strangers while I thought we were on a date, talk about guys in her classes that she "wouldn't mind fucking." She'd told me about her no-relationship policy on our first date, so I guess I should have known better.

The bullshit with Darcy continued, though I guess I got used to him hanging around. He apologized for the penknife incident, but he was constantly making fun of me and was still a first-rate prick. The more I saw him with Melanie the less I saw him as competition. They were more like rival siblings or kissing cousins. Harmless.

About three weeks after Halloween I had my first legitimate

conversation with Darcy. Melanie told me to meet her at The Bloody Paw for nachos. I'd spent the day collecting dead mice from the boiler room at Our Lady of Sorrows, Frayne's only Catholic school. Melanie said to come straight from work, but I went home briefly to shower and change out of my uniform. I suspected Darcy would be there and I was right. The two of them were sitting in one of the booths by the window. They had a pitcher of beer and were digging into an enormous chili-cheese platter.

"Better order your own," Darcy said.

I took a seat at the edge of the booth and, when the waitress came around, ordered an Adios Motherfucker.

Melanie unleashed a roaring belch and patted her chest.

"Nice!" Darcy said, snapping his fingers gangsta-style.

Melanie winked.

Darcy exhaled through puffed cheeks. "This chili is making me sweat!" He shook off his hoodie and resumed his feast in a ratty wife-beater. I'd never noticed before: his upper body was covered in tattoos, everything from barbed-wire armbands and sailor's anchors to pornographic cartoon women with round breasts and jutting asses. Just below his throat was a small Mexican skull. On his left shoulder, in dark black ink, was the symbol for Anarchy, and on his right, a big green crucifix made of rose stems with blood dripping from the thorns. I tried not to stare.

"Got any smokes?" Melanie asked, fanning her mouth with a greasy napkin.

Darcy shrugged.

"I'll grab some," Melanie said. She climbed out of the booth and almost kneed me in the groin in the process. "What brand do you want?"

"Whatever, fuck," Darcy said.

I watched as he lifted his plate and swept nacho crumbs and cheese bits into his mouth with the side of his hand.

"Nice tats," I said.

He nodded, licking his fingers. "You got any?"

"Me? No."

He chuckled a bit. "Mel's blank too. She thinks tattoos clash with freckles. I say it depends on the design. Plus, there's nothing sexier than an inked-up ginger bitch, am I right?"

The waitress arrived with my drink. Darcy picked it up and took a sip without a word. I let it slide.

"The thing about tattoos," he went on, "is that nobody takes them seriously. They're on your skin for *life*, know what I'm saying? Be aware! Some douchebag goes to Thailand and gets a few Asian symbols needled into his shoulder 'cause he thinks they look cool, only he doesn't realize he's advertising himself as a syphilitic ass-monkey. Serves him right. You gotta think about that shit. Look, right here." He pulled down the neck of his tank top and exposed a question mark on his left bicep with the Mars astrological symbol for a dot. "I got this one as a representation of my bastardhood."

I squinted. "What do you mean, 'bastardhood'?"

"Bastardhood, idiot! I never knew my father. He's a mystery to me. I'm a motherfucking bastard, in all senses of the word."

"What about those women? What are they, characters from your favourite Japanese animation?"

His eyes widened as he took another sip of my drink. "Holy shit," he said, swallowing. "That's exactly what they are. They're hentai. You heard of it?"

I shook my head.

"You should check it out. It's all over the Internet. You

strike me as the kind of guy who looks at porn. I bet you masturbate with strict regularity."

I couldn't help but laugh. His verbal assaults were only offensive for so long. Once you got used to them they became funny in a way that made *him* the joke. I began to see why Melanie might want him around. He was like a clown whose role was merely to shock and amuse his friends. Perhaps that was his only way of making friends.

"What about the ones on your shoulders?" I asked.

He leaned forward, dropped his arms, and flexed his puny boy-muscles. "Christian Anarchy, baby," he said. "It's what I'm *about*."

"What's that? Some kind of Jesus-meets-Johnny-Rotten hybrid faith?"

"That's an ignorant way of putting it, but basically yes. Jesus was the first and only real anarchist the world has ever known. He said fuck the status quo and told things like they really were. Then the church came along and messed everything up. It's nothing but a goddamn beaurocracy between man and God, is what it is. Luke seventeen, twenty-one: 'the kingdom of God is within you.'" He thumped his hand against his rib-ridged chest. "That's all I know, and all I *need* to know."

"Interesting," I said. "So you're a religious guy?"

He guzzled the rest of my drink. "In a matter of speaking. I don't believe in religion as a path to God. The way I see it, no path is required because He's already fucking there. He's *everywhere*. Jesus tried to tell people that, only they're too dumb to get it. They think it's gotta be complicated, but it isn't. It's the easiest thing in the world: pure . . . fucking . . . freedom. Governments and the church are nothing but smoke and mirrors. The individual's the only thing that's holy. Anything else is a golden calf."

I have to admit I was impressed. I didn't expect a slimeball like Darcy to be so articulate about his beliefs, or so passionate about *anything*.

He turned and looked out the window, which made me look as well. Melanie was huddled under an awning, trying to light a cigarette despite the November wind.

Darcy stood up and slung on his hoodie. "Excuse me, but I need to increase my chances of developing lung cancer."

I signalled to the waitress for the bill and she brought it over right away. I slapped down forty bucks to cover the nachos and drinks, none of which I'd actually consumed — my Christian deed for the day.

Outside, Melanie and Darcy were lighting up a second round of smokes, so I took a seat at the bar and picked through the dish of breath mints. As I was about to grab the sole red candy in a cluster of greens, a voice to my left said, "Brandon? No kidding!"

I turned and saw Bill. He was sitting alone at the end of the bar with his gut hanging over his belt like a flabby anaesthetized tongue.

"What are you doing here?" I asked him.

He wrapped his hand around the pint glass in front of him. "Having a beer, what else?"

"Do you come here often?"

"What, are you trying to pick me up or something?" he wheezed.

"Funny, it's just . . . This doesn't strike me as your kind of place."

"Are you kidding me? I love this joint." He spread out his arms. "I mean, come on. Look at all the beautiful pictures they got. That one there was donated by yours truly, I'm proud to say." He nodded at a particularly gruesome close-up of a blood-caked paw that had been crudely severed from the limb of its former owner. It was small, like a cub's paw. It might well have been the shot that inspired the bar's name.

"Jesus."

Bill crossed his arms and stuck out his chin as though admiring the showpiece in an art gallery. "Beautiful, isn't it?"

"Please tell me you're joking."

"I'm a hunter, Brandon. It's in my blood. My dad, and his dad, and his dad, and so on — the Barbers are a hunting clan. Real men, from an earlier age." He laughed at his own joke. "I guess you could say we hunt for a living, you and I. But squishing spiders just doesn't compare to blowing a hole in a grizzly's rib cage, know what I mean? That crunch of bone, that echo-y bear roar. Feeling its pain vibrate in your own body."

I stared.

"You gotta experience it to know what I mean," he said.

"You know this place is run by an environmentalist," I said. "It's anti-hunting."

"Viktor? Shit." He looked from side to side and leaned in close. "Between you and me, Viktor don't care about animals. He's looking to make a buck and get laid in the process, same as the next guy. These university babes eat that bleeding-heart shit right up."

"I guess."

"Listen, I'll let you get back to your girl out there. See you back at work tomorrow. Those mice won't know what hit 'em. Whap!" He smacked his hands together loudly.

"Take it easy, Bill," I said, and went outside in a haze.

"You okay?" Melanie asked as she stamped out her cigarette. "You look kind of pale."

"I'll be all right. I can only take so much of this place."

POISON SHY

Darcy got in a cab to check out some new slasher film at the movieplex outside of town. He tried to convince Melanie to go but she said she needed to study for a test.

"What's your test on?" I asked, after Darcy's cab had sped away.

"You're not very bright, are you?" She giggled. "Your place or mine?"

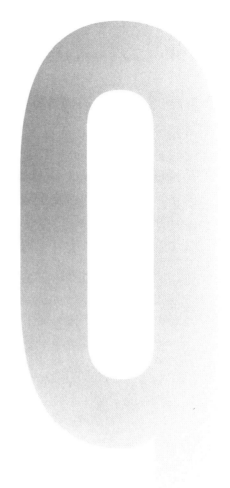

Three days later I felt the burn.

I knew something was wrong when I woke in the middle of the night to pee, like an old man with an inflamed prostate.

Too tired to stand and aim, I sat on the toilet and waited. There was a dull ache in my kidneys. Now that I was here, out of bed and on the toilet, I couldn't seem to go. I closed my eyes and coaxed the urine through. An acid sting flared at the tip of my penis as I spilled into the toilet.

I went back to bed and dreamed I was sliding along a conveyor belt, naked and with my penis fully erect, waiting my turn for a sandpaper scrubbing.

When I woke for work I had to pee again. Urgently. But like before, it didn't come whizzing out like it seemed to want to. I planted my feet firmly on either side of my floor mat and pushed with all my might. I needed *something* to flow through my urethra to alleviate the pinched soreness, the grainy ache.

When I started to think I might shit myself standing up, a slow dribble of dark orange bladder juice sprinkled into the toilet. It felt like someone had shoved a splintered popsicle stick inside me.

"What the fuck?" I stood there, perplexed. Everything looked normal. My penis wasn't scabby or blackening or about to fall off; no yellow slime oozing from the glans. But that needing-to-go sensation had actually become more intense.

I put on a pair of tighty-whiteys. There was something soothing about having my package held snugly inside the stretchable fabric pouch. I left a quick message on KEA'S answering machine saying I wouldn't be in due to a personal emergency, then called for a cab. Told the dispatcher to hurry it up because my dick was on fire. He said he understood completely. The taxi arrived within minutes.

The only walk-in clinic I knew of was on the west side of town, near my mother's place, in a cracked building above a pharmacy that was only open at night. I ran up the stairs and into the small waiting room. The doctor and receptionist stood chatting by the check-in desk. The woman quickly removed her hand from the doctor's crotch area and blushed. The doctor cleared his throat.

"Can I get an appointment, please?" I said.

They looked at me like I was a stray dog who'd come bounding in, barking for attention. Some dumb animal that can neither recognize nor appreciate the subtleties of illicit human courtship.

"What seems to be the problem?" the doctor asked after I'd signed in and we were alone in his windowless office.

"I think I have a bladder infection. It stings when I pee and I seem to have to go badly all the time, even after I've just gone."

"Let's have a look." He snapped on a pair of plastic gloves.

I stood up and unzipped. His hands were cold and alien on my prick.

"Is the pain concentrated at the tip?" he asked.

"Sort of. It's pretty irritated everywhere, but the tip hurts most when I pee."

He told me to lay down on my back on the bed coated with waxed paper and proceeded to shove a Q-tip into my piss-hole.

"It'll take about a week for the test results to come in," he said as he snapped the swab into a little plastic tube, "but my guess is you have chlamydia. Have you had unprotected sex recently?"

A concrete ball formed in my stomach. My vision blurred and I thought I might black out. He might as well have told me I had a week to live.

"Well?"

I had to really concentrate. I stuck my knuckles deep into my eye sockets and rubbed. "Umm, yes, I have, actually."

He tore a page from his prescription pad and started scribbling. "That's probably it. I recommend you see your family doctor as soon as possible to get tested for other STIs. In the meantime I'll write you a script for some antibiotics. Oh, and make sure you contact anyone you've had sexual contact with recently. Within the last month or two."

I needed to be comforted so I went to my mother's. I wanted to cry on her shoulder and have her tell me I wasn't a bad person. I wanted her to say that I was a nice young man who'd had a bit of bad luck, and that everybody — even the Pope — makes mistakes.

I found her bundled in her blanket like a tumorous pumpkin, whispering to herself about the spiritual filthiness of humanity.

"I've missed you, Brandon," she said. "You haven't been to see me in a while."

Visiting her turned out to be the right thing, but not because she comforted me. I didn't even tell her about the chlamydia. Her wild hair, bloodshot eyes, and stinking woollen cloak made my illness seem trivial. It was curable. I told her I'd taken the day off because I missed her too, and wanted to buy her lunch. I ordered some Chinese and as we ate the discomfort in my crotch subsided. I hadn't even taken a pill. I told her about Melanie and the mouse problem at the Catholic school.

"How terrible," she said.

"I know. Those poor kids —"

"No, I mean the girl. She's not right for you, Brandon."

"What?" I said, laughing. "Mom, you don't know anything about her."

"I know she's too young for you. And probably a slut. They're all sluts these days."

The pain in my crotch made a fierce return. I scratched my stubbly cheeks. "She's not a slut."

"I think you should stay away from her. Women bring nothing but pain to a man. If your father were alive he'd tell you the same thing. You should think about joining the seminary. It's never too late, you know. You'd make a lovely deacon."

I excused myself and unleashed four excruciating drips into my mother's toilet. After we finished lunch I went to the nearest pharmacy.

Melanie wasn't answering her phone. I must have called her twenty times. She's probably fucking a gigolo, I thought. Picking up something else to pass along. I thought about our first night together and got furious. She'd basically raped me. Infected me. The timeline was off for the hooker to be responsible, and she'd only given me a blowjob anyway.

It could only have been Melanie. She didn't have voicemail so I couldn't leave a message. I wrote her an email instead.

Identity: b_galloway@kea.com
To: ginger_sex_kitten@sparkmail.net
Cc:
Bcc:
Subject: important

Melanie — call me as soon as you get this. I've been
to the doctor and I think you've given me the clap.
Have you been tested lately? I need to hear from
you!

Brandon

I popped one of the antibiotics, plus a Tylenol with codeine. Washed them down with a mug of yesterday's coffee. My phone rang while I was taking yet another painful whiz. I ran out of my bathroom with my pants at my ankles. It was Chad.

"Dude, where you been? I've been trying to get in touch with you for days."

"Hey, man. What's up?"

"Well, nothing really. Ha! I just hadn't heard from you since you went on that date and I thought, I bet Brandon is

chin-deep in pussy right now. I bet he has his cock pushed to
the hilt inside that redhead's slip-and-slide. You're probably
fucking her as we speak, aren't you? Don't lie."

I held the phone away from my ear.

"You there, Brandon?"

"Yeah, I'm here. Listen, Chad — I know I've been MIA lately,
but I've got a lot of shit going on. To be honest with you, I
think that chick gave me an STD. I'm kind of freaking out here.
She's not answering her phone."

"Are you serious?" There was a pause. "That bitch. That
fucking *bitch*. You want me to hunt her down? I told you
Farah's old man's a cop, right?"

"Take it easy, okay? I don't need the cops, for God's sake. I'm
not one-hundred-percent sure about anything yet. That's why I
have to get in touch with her. I have to let you go, all right? I'll
give you a call when I know what the hell is going on."

I turned on the TV. Distracted myself for a while with a show
in which two idiot friends competed to see who could get the
most phone numbers from women at the mall, and the loser had
to eat a spoonful of his friend's shit. The winner secretly took a
laxative to make matters worse for his humiliated companion.

At the end of the show someone buzzed my apartment.

"Who's there?" I blurted into the speaker.

"Jessica Rabbit," Melanie said. "I came to pick up my booby
trap."

I buzzed her in and tried on angry faces in the mirror.
None of them were intimidating. I looked more constipated
than pissed.

She thumped up the stairs and strolled casually through my
door wearing sex-red lipstick and a pair of oversized sunglasses.
Four large paper bags hung from her wrists, all of them filled

with new clothes and feminine products. She blew me a kiss, then squeaked out a fart as she bent to place her bags on the floor. "Oops. That was Taco Bell."

"We have to talk."

"That sounds like the intro to a breakup." She walked into my kitchen, swinging her hips, and opened the fridge. Took out a jar of sliced pickles and dropped one into her mouth from above, dripping brine onto her shirt. "Don't you have to be dating to break up?"

"No joking around. This is serious." I put my hands in my pockets. "I think you gave me the clap."

"Gonorrhea?"

"What? *Gonorrhea*? No, the clap. Chlamydia."

She smiled condescendingly. "The clap is gonorrhea, sweetheart. Get your STI facts straight before you go accusing people of infecting you."

"Whatever. I woke up this morning with a sore-as-hell dick that burns every time I take a piss, so I went to the doctor and he said he thinks I have chlamydia. You're the only person I've slept with in years, so . . ."

"Did you get your test results?"

"No, but —"

"You're such an asshole."

"*I'm* an asshole? Me?"

She moved toward me. "Let me see your cock."

"*Excuse me*? You're not going anywhere near it, thanks."

"I didn't give you chlamydia, Brandon."

"When's the last time you were tested?"

"I don't know. Last year. I usually always use a condom."

"*Usually* always? What the hell does that mean?"

"Calm down and let me think."

POISON
SHY

"I'll tell you what it means. It means you *don't* always use a condom, Melanie." I sat down and sighed. "Christ, I'm such an idiot."

"Stop talking and let me think." She sat down beside me. Her cheeks were flushed, her body warm. She smelled like cloves and candle wax — the scent reminded me of when I first set foot in her bedroom.

I looked at her as she sat thinking: lips pursed, brow furrowed, freckles everywhere. Hair so orange it glowed, even in the dim lighting. Suddenly I wanted to throw myself at her feet and beg her painted toenails for forgiveness.

"Let me see," she said, chewing on her pinkie. "Dylan always used a condom. Tommy had a premature ejaculation issue. I don't think he was ever technically inside me. Viktor was more into domination than actual sex, and even when he did fuck me he always wore one. There's Isabel — but a girl can't get chlamydia from another girl, can she? I honestly can't think who it could be." She swallowed. "Unless . . ."

"Unless what?"

"Darcy."

"You've slept with Darcy?"

"Duh."

"I knew it!"

"Uh, yeah."

"How many times have you —"

"Fuck, I don't know! You think I keep track? God, you're such a *loser!*"

"You think you might have caught it from him?"

"Well, I still don't think I have it, but it's a possibility. I guess I'll get tested."

"You haven't noticed any symptoms?"

"Nope."

"No itching or burning?"

"I said no."

I threw open the fridge and got a beer. Melanie brought her shopping bags to the couch and began sorting through her stuff, completely unperturbed. She was humming a pop song.

I drank half the bottle of beer and stared at her from the kitchen doorway. "I can't believe you slept with Darcy."

"Get over it."

"He probably has HIV from all those tattoos."

She bit the price tag off a pink thong. "I guess we're both gonna die then."

"I'm not kidding, Melanie."

"Neither am I."

"I thought you two were just friends."

"We were. We *are*. We're also two young people of the opposite sex who live under the same roof. We drink, we get bored and horny. Things happen."

"When did 'things' first happen?"

"Jesus, Brandon, who cares?"

"I care."

"You know, I never would have thought you'd be the jealous type."

"I'm not jealous. I just can't see why you'd want to fuck someone so disgusting."

"*You're* disgusting, you know that?"

"Me?"

"Your jealousy disgusts me. There's nothing more repulsive."

There was a keen silence. A car passed outside. My lamp-shade rattled. Melanie continued to sort through clothes. I downed another beer and told her I was going for a walk. Asked her if she wanted anything. She ignored me.

I put on my jacket and walked the streets. When I got

POISON
SHY

hungry I went to a pizza place and ordered a large pepperoni with extra cheese. Melanie was getting out of the shower when I got back. We ate together in front of the TV — me still in my jacket and shoes, Melanie in flannel pyjamas with a towel wrapped around her head like a turban — and watched *Late Night with Conan O'Brien*. His second guest was a sex expert. They joked about birth control and STDs. I turned off the TV and told Melanie she could sleep in my bed as long as she didn't touch me. She said she wouldn't even dream of it.

Half an hour later I rolled on a condom and fucked her doggie-style with her face pressed into a pillow.

I woke, took a leak. It hurt less. The antibiotics were kicking in.

Melanie got up a few minutes after the coffee was made. She asked if she could have a cigarette in my kitchen. I said why not. We sat together like an old married couple and ate peanut butter and jelly sandwiches. It was all very sweet until she decided to turn the breakfast table into a confessional.

"When I met Darcy I was attracted to him right away. He was in our common room going shot for shot with a huge exchange student from Denmark. He drank the guy under the table, made him look like the biggest pussy. The dude ending up puking on Darcy's shoes, and Darcy made him lick it off in front of everybody. I think I fell in love right then. I got drunk, went back to his dorm. He didn't seem interested, though, which only made me want him more. He kept me up all night yapping about Jesus when all I could think about was how bad I wanted to go down on him. He didn't have the most attractive face in the world, but there was something about him. Charisma, I guess. He was the most popular guy in rez. A party animal who got straight As without ever going to class. Treated everybody like shit and still they loved him. He liked me for some reason, though. He said I had the same ideals as him, I was just too dumb to know it. I tried to fuck him so many times, but no matter how drunk he got he wouldn't touch me. I knew he wasn't gay because he'd slept with a few of the other girls, and anyway, I could just tell. By the end of first year we were pretty good friends, and I convinced him to get a place with me off campus. I'd purposely walk around the apartment in my bra and panties, make him dinner, do his laundry, all that stuff. I could feel him watching me and it turned me on, but nothing ever happened. I went out with a few guys and I know it bugged him. He'd get drunk and wait for me to come home."

She stubbed out her smoke and lit another. "Finally, one night, after I'd passed out on my bed in a G-string, he came into my room and started licking my asshole. I have no idea how long he was going at it before I woke up. It was so weird, but I thought, at least he finally gave in. We messed around and he ended up putting it in my ass." She paused and looked at me. Blew a couple smoke rings. "No guy had ever done that to me before. I didn't mind. It wasn't the greatest thing, but Darcy loved it. It's all he ever wanted to do. We got into this routine where, if I came home on the weekend without a guy,

Darcy would come into my room, make me suck his dick for a while, then fuck me in the ass. At one point he got a pretty bad bladder infection and stuff kind of stopped. We slipped back into our old ways, our friendship before the sex. Then I met you and he started creeping around again, but I'd just laugh. I couldn't take him seriously. I guess I didn't love him anymore."

I swallowed a thick clump of peanut butter and toast. Felt it slug down my throat, dry as a hairball. What the fuck was I supposed to say? What was I supposed to *think*?

Melanie snorted. "When I saw you at the library with your little orange, reeking of whisky, I thought, this guy needs to get laid. Darcy hadn't touched me in weeks. He was obsessed with this skinny blonde girl Sarah in his philosophy class and I guess I was feeling a little spurned. I didn't know anything about you, but you sort of reminded me of Darcy. Don't get me wrong, you're way better looking. It's weird, though. There's something about you two that's similar."

"I think I'm going to be sick," I said.

"I didn't even really like you," she said. "I just wanted to piss off Darcy. But when we went on our date I could tell you were really into me. You were, like, nervous. It was pathetic, but kind of sweet. Usually guys just want to fuck me. You seemed like you'd rather snuggle up on the couch and watch a movie. Bizarre. You were also afraid of me. I liked that too."

"I don't want to hear any more."

"Just listen. After our date, I could tell Darcy was jealous. He wouldn't admit it, though. I thought I'd be happy about it but I wasn't. He turned into an asshole — not the usual ass-hole Darcy, but a real fucking prick. Whining all the time and insulting me to my face. Maybe that's the way he'd always been and I just couldn't see it, I don't know. Anyway, that keg party was the last straw. I found my way to your place and you let me in. Let me sleep in your bed. I woke up at one point and saw you asleep in your chair. I watched you for a while. You looked so uncomfortable! There was a piece of fluff on your nose that fluttered back and forth as you breathed. Your face was all scrunched up. It was bugging the hell out of you but you couldn't wipe it off. It was so cute, and a perfect snapshot of who you are — oblivious and helpless."

"I'm glad you think so highly of me."

"I do, you idiot! That's what I'm trying to tell you."

"You realize I'm going to punch Darcy in the face next time I see him."

"Right. And I'm a virgin."

I've read it a number of times in self-help books: we place the most trust in those who are most likely to deceive us. It's not that I believed or trusted Melanie about her feelings for me. As a matter of fact, I didn't trust her at all. My problem was that I *wanted* to — and in my experience, desire not only trumps logic, it scratches it out completely.

A few days after Melanie's testimonial, I went to a lock shop, got my apartment key duplicated, and gave it to her. Like most idiots, I was riding a wave of positivity in the aftermath of disappointment. I even looked forward to seeing Darcy so I could look into his jaundiced eyes, have a good laugh at his ridiculous perversions, and move on. It seemed I'd won the girl. Sure, my soul — which I wasn't even sure existed — had been ripped up and crudely Scotch-taped back together in the process . . . but hey, that's courtship.

The following Saturday I had dinner with Chad and Farah at East Side Mario's. I invited Melanie along, but she wasn't feeling well. It turned out she did have chlamydia, just not the symptoms. The antibiotics made her nauseous. I, on the other hand, was almost completely healed. There was no more pain, just a vague discomfort, and only for the first piss of the day.

"You're one lucky bastard," Chad said, with a mouth full of garlic bread. "You could've got AIDS."

"Don't freak him out," Farah said. "He's been through enough."

"It's no big deal, really," I told them. "Aside from the day it hit me, it wasn't too painful. I think I caught it early. I was more ashamed than anything. When you learn about these things in sex ed, you think they only happen to prostitutes and porn stars. I thought I'd go my whole life without even *knowing* anyone with an STD. It was a reality check."

"So you've forgiven her, then?" Farah asked. "I think that's romantic."

"Romantic?" Chad snorted. "Can you pass the Parmesan?"

"I wouldn't say I've forgiven her," I said. "More like we're working through it."

Chad pitchforked his rigatoni. "Hey — they're your balls."

When I got back to my apartment, I found two empty beer bottles on my coffee table. The door to my closet was open and the thermostat had been changed. My fridge had been left open a crack, too. I had to throw out a tub of yogurt and a carton of milk.

I flopped onto my couch and cracked a lukewarm beer. Read the first few chapters of Edith Wharton's *Ethan Frome*, a book Melanie had left at my place. She was supposed to be reading it for school but said it was "boring as shit."

Around eleven my phone rang. The call display said *Frayne Police Dept.*

I let it ring five or six times before answering.

"Mr. Brandon Galloway?" said the gruff and vaguely foreign voice on the other end.

"Yes."

"This is Detective Basil Darvish. I have a Mr. Darcy Sands and a Miss Melanie Blaxley here at the station. They say they know you."

"I . . . Yes, I know them. Can I ask what —"

"And you work for Kill All of Them pest control services, is that correct?"

"I work for Kill 'Em All, yes."

"I'd like you to come down to the station. Tonight. Can you be here in fifteen minutes?"

"I don't understand what —"

"Bring photo ID, please. Fifteen minutes." He hung up.

It was about a twenty-five minute walk to the police station from my apartment. Instead of calling a cab I jogged all the way there, whispering the phrase "You didn't do anything wrong" over and over again, though I wasn't sure I believed it.

I got to the station, took a few deep breaths, and went inside. Melanie and Darcy were sitting in the lobby playing cards like they were in their own living room.

"Hey," Melanie said blandly.

Darcy met my gaze for a second, then turned back to his hand. He was wearing my Kill 'Em All uniform. It looked like a baggy straightjacket on him.

"Mr. Galloway?" said a voice behind me.

I turned to see a tall, olive-skinned man with short, curly black hair and a stubbly, greying beard. He wore a pair of chalky old cargo pants and a navy blue sweater vest. His eyes were bulbous and penetrating. His hands were enormous.

"Detective Basil Darvish," he said, approaching me. "I appreciate you coming."

"Can we go now?" Darcy said from across the room.

Darvish ignored him. "I just spoke with my daughter," he said to me. "She says she knows you. Her name is Farah."

"Oh, yeah. She knows my friend Chad."

Darvish nodded, then gestured toward Melanie and Darcy. "I caught these two breaking into a home this evening. Mr. Sands was posing as an exterminator. He later confessed that the uniform he's wearing belongs to you."

"Oh jeez."

"Didn't you notice it was missing?"

"No, Officer. I didn't."

Darvish cleared his throat. "It's Detective, Mr. Galloway. Please."

"Sorry, Detective."

Melanie and Darcy had stopped their game and were looking at us.

"I'm trying to give these two a break here," Darvish said. "I don't think they've gotten that through their thick skulls. Forgive me for being skeptical, but the uniform has the name Dennis stitched on it. I trust you brought some identification?"

I handed him my whole wallet, which contained my KEA ID, a bus pass, some grocery receipts, and an expired driver's licence. He flipped through it, scratching his scruff. I think he even glanced at how much cash I had in there.

"I suggest you take better care of your professional belongings, Mr. Galloway," he said. "Of course it wouldn't be appropriate for me to suggest you take better care when choosing friends."

"Are they being charged with anything?" I asked.

Darvish stood stone-still with his hands in his pockets. "The individual whose home they invaded has decided not to press charges."

"Can we go now?" Darcy said.

Darvish took a hand out of his pocket and gestured toward the exit without a word. He was looking at me for some reason, not the two morons he'd apprehended.

"What the fuck happened?" I asked when we got outside.

"Darcy's a pervert, that's what," Melanie said.

"*I'm* the pervert? Excuse *me*, Miss Golden Shower —"

"That has nothing to do with this," Melanie snapped.

"Will you two shut up and tell me what happened?"

They looked at each other, then burst out laughing.

"It's stupid," Melanie said. "Darcy was telling me about Sarah, that girl from his philosophy class. Apparently she has this rape fantasy —"

"Shut up, I'll tell the story," Darcy said. "This girl Sarah, she's a strange one — ultra-conservative, hates feminism, thinks it's responsible for what she calls the 'pansification' of the modern male, the decline of traditional family values, *et cetera*. She likes it when men assert their dominance. Thinks misogyny will lead society back into Eden. She believes so deeply in these things that they've infiltrated her sexual preferences. The other day she confessed to me that if a man ever broke into her apartment to rape her, she'd let him have his way with her. She said she might even enjoy it."

"What a sick fuck," Melanie said. "Personally, I'd bite off the guy's testicles."

"Will you let me tell the story? Anyway, we were sitting around the apartment, bored off our asses —"

"Speak for yourself," Melanie said.

"Will you shut the fuck up for one second please? God. *Anyway*, I was bored as shit, so I thought it would be a good time to put Sarah's claim to the test. There's nothing I like more than exposing people for the frauds they really are. I didn't actually want to rape her, just scare her a little. See how she reacted. I knew Melanie had a key to your place, so while she was busy painting her toenails, I borrowed her key-chain and told her I was going to Sarah's. I knew you weren't home because when I asked Melanie why she was at home instead of sucking your dick, she said you were having dinner with friends."

"Wait," I said. "How did you know where I live?"

Darcy laughed and shook his head. "You think I don't know where you live?"

"I followed him because I knew something was fishy," Melanie said.

"So you broke into my house and stole my uniform." My hands were shaking. "Maybe I should press charges too."

"Technically he didn't break in," Melanie said. "I caught up to him when I realized where he was going, and I let us both in."

"What the fuck for?"

"So he could break into that bitch's house dressed as a bug guy and scare the shit out of her, that's why," Melanie said. "I hate that little slut. She spread rumours about me in first year. Told everyone I was a walking STD."

"How prophetic," Darcy said.

"Fuck you."

"What the hell did you need the uniform for?" I said.

"For effect," Darcy said. "Spice the fantasy up a bit."

I looked at Melanie. "And you went along with this?"

"I already told you. I can't stand the bitch."

"You two are unbelievable, you know that?" I quickened my pace.

"Don't you want to know what happened?"

What happened was this: Melanie let Darcy into my place so he could "borrow" my uniform. Darcy also "borrowed" a few of my beers — not for liquid courage but liquid aggression, as he put it. Then they went over to Sarah's place, a mouldy old six-bedroom mansion she shared with five other girls. Darcy knew that Sarah's bedroom was located on the main floor. He also knew that Jill, Sarah's anorexic roommate, liked to crank up the heat. Because of this, Sarah would often keep her bedroom window open, though she kept the curtains drawn, especially at night. Melanie and Darcy crept into the backyard. Sure enough, Sarah's window was open. They could hear her belting out Cyndi Lauper's "Girls Just Want to Have Fun" from the other side of the curtains.

At this point in the story, Melanie chimed in to say that after hearing Sarah butcher such a classic, she hoped Darcy wound up raping her for real. She hoisted Darcy up through the window. Someone in the room screamed, but it wasn't Sarah. It was her roommate Jill, all eighty-nine pounds of her, with soaking wet hair and a towel wrapped around her naked body. Darcy stared at her with a half-erection jutting out from the crotch of *my* uniform. Jill continued to scream. One of Sarah's other roommates appeared, took one look at the scene, and called 911. Darcy and Melanie were sitting in the back of a cop car by the time Sarah, who'd had dibs on the shower after Jill, even knew what was going on.

"She must have calmed her roomies down and told them she'd invited me over or something," Darcy said. "Then told Detective Dipshit there were no charges to press."

"You realize I will never wear that uniform again," I said.

Darcy raised his ratty eyebrow. "You got a problem with my dick cheese?"

Melanie bent over laughing.

I stuffed my hands in my pockets and left the idiots in the street.

"Explain it to me again," my boss Dick said. "Just so I'm clear."

"My girlfriend's idiot friend broke into my home, stole my uniform, and almost got himself arrested for unlawful entry."

"And *why* isn't the uniform back in your possession?"

"Because . . ." I cleared my throat. "Because while he was wearing it he got an erection."

Dick stood up and rested his knuckles on his desk. "Let me get this straight. Some perverted muttonhead stole your uniform and was so jacked by his little game of dress-up that he got a raging hard-on and mucked up the inside of your duds?"

"That's basically what happened, yes."

"You expect me to believe that bunk?"

"It's true, I —"

"Get the fuck out of my office, Brandon. Starting now you're on an unpaid leave of absence until I decide whether or not to fire your ass."

"But Dick —"

"Now go home and have a shower, for Christ's sake. You look like hell."

Bad decisions. That's what it came down to. Getting involved with Melanie was a bad decision. Giving Darcy the benefit of the doubt was a bad decision — he truly was a terrorist in the making. Getting a job at Kill 'Em All seemed like a bad decision, because I wouldn't have met them otherwise. Being born in the first place wasn't a bad decision on my part, but I could easily blame that one on my parents.

Humanity was God's bad decision, plain and simple.

When I got to my apartment, I found Melanie's key on my coffee table next to a post-it note. *I think it's time for a break*, it said. No apology, no admission of guilt, nothing.

I went to the bathroom and splashed cold water on my face. My phone rang, but I wasn't in the mood to speak to anyone. My machine picked it up and I heard a woman's voice say, "Hello, this is Saint Aiden's Hospital calling for Mr. Brandon Galloway. Your mother had an accident and was brought to emergency. She's okay, but, ah, she doesn't seem to want to accept our help, and . . . Well, you were listed as her emergency contact person. Please come to the hospital as soon as you get this."

Was all of this really happening at once?

I stared into the sink and actually started laughing. My

mother was lying in a hospital bed and I was staring down a drain hole, tittering like a circus clown. I poured some beer into a thermos and drank it on the bus on the way to Saint Aiden's.

The woman at the reception desk literally pinched her nose when I told her I'd come to see Eileen Galloway.

"Room 309. Elevator's down the hall."

Some big lug stepped into the elevator behind me. It wasn't until I'd pushed the button for the third floor that I noticed he was hospital security. The receptionist must have put him on my trail.

I found room 309 and went inside, afraid of what I might find. My mother was propped up in her bed, flanked by pillows and — what else? — the orange blanket. Her half-closed eyes were glued to the little TV that sat on a shelf on the wall. She didn't look at me, but I knew she knew I was there. When I sat down beside her I noticed she was strapped to the bed like a mental patient — which I suppose she was, now. It had finally come to that.

"What happened, Mom?"

"They want my organs, I know it," she said. "They want to cut me open and sell my insides to inspectors, spies, and Satan's minions."

"Don't be ridiculous, Ma. What happened? Did you fall?"

She moved her arms around under the straps. They were wrapped in bandages up to her elbows.

Tears welled up in my eyes, but I fought them back with everything I had. "Did you do something to yourself?"

She looked at me. Her eyes were weak and full of the pain of a tortured existence. "How am I supposed to live, Brandon? Tell me how."

It wasn't a rhetorical question. My mother never knew how to live. I was beginning to think that I didn't either.

POISON SHY

The security guard paced the hall outside.

"You'll be okay," I said, swallowing the lump in my throat. "These people are going to take care of you better than I can."

"I don't trust them. I don't trust anyone."

With all of my heart I wanted to say *Neither do I*. Instead I said, "I love you, Mom."

She gestured for the cup of water on her bedside table. I held it to her mouth as she drank.

"I want you to know something," she said. "It's about your father. Something he left behind before he died."

"What are you talking about?"

"I didn't want you to know, but you have to. You have to know. Your father hurt me badly. Sinned his heart out all his life. But you have to remember that love takes no pleasure in other people's sins, but delights in the truth. You have to know the truth, Brandon."

"Jeez, Ma."

"There was a woman named Gloria Sands."

I stopped breathing. *Sands.* That name . . .

"She was your father's mistress. Well, one of his mistresses."

"Mom —"

"I found out about the affair on your eighth birthday. I went to her house, Brandon. I went to her house to kill her."

"Mom. Please."

She started crying, and I realized I was crying too.

"I couldn't do it," she said. "Not after I saw her. I just couldn't. She was pregnant with your father's child."

My vision blurred. I stood up quickly. Reached into my coat pocket for the thermos and spilled it all over the floor.

That was enough for the security guard. He stormed in and tried to tackle me. I swerved to avoid him and slipped on the beer on the floor. My head hit something hard. The last thing I remember before going unconscious is the look of pity on the guard's fat face.

I woke up on a stretcher in an empty room. My clothes were still on, but my shoes had been taken off and placed on the bedside table to my right. I could smell them.

When I sat up, I could almost hear the blood rushing out of my head. I touched the back of my skull and felt something gauzy and wet. My fingers came away red. I didn't need a mirror to show me that my head was wrapped in a turban of blood-soggy bandages.

I needed to get out of the hospital and find Gloria Sands. Frayne was a small town, but not so small that this Gloria was necessarily my father's former mistress, or even Darcy's mother for that matter. It was all a coincidence and I wanted to prove it.

I opened the door and poked my head out into the hall. Nothing but a few whistling orderlies, a bare-assed old man hooked up to a drip stand, and the cold stench of sterility and death. I zipped up my jacket and walked casually to the elevator. Pushed the down button and waited for the security guard to tap me on the shoulder.

When I stepped into the elevator and watched the doors close without anyone else getting on, I knew I was free. The doors opened in the lobby and I strolled out of there with my hands in my pockets, nodding at the bare-legged smokers and wheelchair-ridden vegetables, sympathizing with them, feeling like a member of their clan.

There was only one Gloria Sands in the phone book, though my source was a water-logged edition I'd found in a public booth. The pages were crunchy and smelled like piss.

Sands, Gloria. 111-57 Malt Rd. 444-5903.

The address was three blocks from the hospital, in an area known to Fraynians as either The Lantern District or Hooker-town.

It was cold, but the weather didn't keep the streetwalkers from doing just that. There were white hookers and black hookers, Asian hookers with small breasts and pert little asses, she-males with fat collagen lips, their packages on display in red leather tights. Goth chicks with tattoos on their faces and fat chicks in ass-less mesh nightgowns. They saw the bandages on my head and shot me sex-hungry looks of compassion, their mothering instincts still alive beneath their skanky exteriors. A teenaged girl in jeans and a bra told me she'd rub both my heads for twenty.

Standing outside Gloria's building, smoking a bitch-stick the length of a pencil, was a buxom redhead in sunglasses and a fur coat. She saw me approaching and smiled. "You looking to spend some time, honey? Ooh, what happened to your noggin?"

"Sorry, not interested." I moved to go inside.

She lowered her sunglasses. "Hang on a second. Darcy?"

I looked at her again. It was Suzie.

"You've got the wrong guy," I said, and pulled the door closed behind me.

There were only eight names on the tenant list in the lobby, all of them single syllables. *Bragg, Ford, Gale, Katz, Sands, Smith, Ward, Wynne.* I punched in the code for Sands, and after a few beeps a crackled voice said, "Who is it?"

"Um, it's, ah . . ." I paused. "This is going to sound crazy but I think you used to know my father. His name was Jack Galloway."

Static.

"Hello?" I said.

"What do you want?"

"Can I come in and talk to you for a second?"

"I don't even know who you are. Goodbye."

"No, please. I need to know if you ever had a son."

Another pause. "What did you say your name was again?"

"It's Brandon. Jack Galloway was my father. Did you know him? Please just let me in."

As I stood in the lobby with my head wrapped in bloody bandages, it occurred to me that the last thing this woman should ever do is let a lunatic like me into her building. It surprised me when the buzzer sounded. I opened the door and made my way down the dark, cabbage-scented hallway to room 111.

The door was ajar. I knocked lightly three times. A calico cat curled around the door and pranced past me down the hall. I knocked two more times. "Hello?"

I heard something like dinner plates clanking together, and a few seconds later the door opened. I saw a yellow-eyed woman with long witchy hair, a mix of grey and sandy blond. She wore a pair of stonewashed jeans and a tank top, exposing a splatter of faded tattoos on her arms and shoulders. She sort of gasped when she saw me, then quickly composed herself.

"Miss Sands?" I asked.

"Jesus Christ, Brandon," she said. "You look so much like your father."

I cleared my throat. "I think your cat escaped."

"Jackie's always escaping," she said. "She likes to wander. It's okay. Do you want to come in?"

Her apartment was small and cramped. There were boxes

of stuff in every corner. The layer of dust on them was thick. Two more cats were curled up on filthy mats under the coffee table. The whole place reeked of cat litter.

"Is your head okay?" she asked. "It looks pretty nasty."

"Just a little accident. I'm all right."

She sat down on her couch with a sigh, and I took the wooden stool across from her. A small TV on a shelf showed a fuzzy episode of *The Sopranos*. I looked around the room for pictures of Darcy, but there was nothing. No pictures at all.

"So you did know my father, then," I said.

She smiled a sad smile, her eyes on the rug. "I did."

"You know, I think I remember you from that bar. What was it called?"

"The Jug," she said. "I remember you too. You were such a cute kid. So quiet and well-behaved. I still work there, you know, only it's not The Jug anymore. Some restaurateur took it over and called it Parker's Grill. Tried to class it up a bit, but nothing's changed. We serve Stella instead of Blue. Big deal."

There was a silence. On the TV, Tony Soprano said, "It was just a little suicidal gesture, that's all."

I could feel Gloria looking at me, but for some reason I didn't want to look at her.

"So tell me," she said. "Why are you sitting in my apartment right now? What is it you want? Most guys who come to this part of town are looking for something . . . specific."

I fidgeted with my shirtsleeve. "I'm not looking for . . . whatever I think you mean."

She crossed her legs. "What do I mean?"

I wasn't interested in playing games. "Did you and my dad have a kid?"

She put her head down and laughed softly. "Is that really why you're here?"

"Of course it is. I thought I said that already."

She rubbed her eyes. "Sorry. I'm sorry. That's right, you did mention that."

"Well?"

"Jack never wanted you to know. He threatened me."

"My dad was an asshole and a drunk. And you know what else? He's dead."

"I know that."

Something scratched at the door. Gloria stood up and let her cat back in. Picked it up and cradled it like a baby. Its purr was laboured. It might've had a lung problem.

"Anything else you want to know?" she asked, a little scornfully.

"Do I know anything yet?"

"God, you're just like your father. Of course we had a kid. A boy."

She didn't need to tell me more. I knew the truth. I reacted with dull acknowledgment, a small step up from indifference. Darcy Sands was my half brother — big fucking deal. In practical terms it meant less than nothing. It didn't even feel like a revelation. More like someone pointing out a mustard stain on your shirt after lunch. On the other hand, something told me there was a storm of shit on the way.

"You okay, Brandon?" Gloria said.

I was surprised to find she was sitting right beside me. The cat was in her lap, and her hand was on my knee.

I nodded. "I should go."

"Please stay," she said. "Have a drink with me."

I looked at her jaundiced eyes, her tattoos. Her breasts sagged almost to her belly.

"I've met Darcy," I said. "I know him. I know him well, actually."

She took her hand away and stood up. "That little bastard sent you here to make a fool out of me, didn't he?"

"No! Miss Sands, that's not what I meant . . ."

She dropped the cat out of her arms and stormed into the kitchen. Opened a drawer and pulled out a steak knife. Pointed it at me. "You better get the fuck out of here."

"Gloria, please! I don't know what I said, but I swear I wasn't sent here."

The cats under the table had been roused awake. They curled around her legs, moaning and mewing as she moved toward me. "You expect me to believe that?"

I stumbled over an empty vase as I backed away. "I didn't know Darcy was your son until just now, I swear. Please put the knife away. I don't even *like* Darcy."

There was a flash of something in her eyes, and I thought she was about to lunge at me. Instead she dropped to her knees with a thud, almost squishing one of her cats in half, and started to cry.

There was nothing I could do but stand there and watch her break down.

"I'm sorry," she bawled. "I'm so, so sorry."

"I'm going to go," I said, but I didn't move.

"He ruined my life. My own little boy . . . ruined my life." She looked at me with desperation. "He's sick, Brandon. He needs help. Probably I do too."

"I don't know what you're talking about," I said. "I'm going now, okay?"

I opened the door. She continued to speak as I speed-walked down the hall.

"He was more than just my son," she yelled. I couldn't make out the rest.

I left Gloria's building through the back door and hopped some fences until I was clear of the Lantern District.

My head throbbed with metronomic consistency. Was I insane, or had Gloria hinted at an incestuous relationship with Darcy? It made me think about Sarah and Abraham, Hera and Zeus, Donny and Marie. I'd gone digging for information and what I got was something out of a tabloid.

As I wandered home, I entertained the thought of suicide for the first time in my twenty-nine years. I'd lost my girlfriend, my job, and a section of my scalp, all in the last twelve hours.

My mother was in the hospital. Darcy was my illegitimate brother, and a sexual deviant to boot. I needed a friend, but more importantly, I needed a drink. No, scratch that. I needed to get boiled as an owl. Chad was probably listening to fuck-me techno and sucking on Farah's toes, but with the night I'd had I was more than willing to disturb him.

I called him as soon as I got home. "Let's get soused," I said when he picked up.

"I don't know, man. Farah and I were gonna stay in and do a movie night."

"Come on, Chad. I'm desperate. I got put on leave at work. I could get fired. My mom's in the hospital. Melanie wants to break up. Did I mention I got put on leave?"

"Jesus. What happened with Melanie?"

"I don't even know, man. Just get your ass over here and let's get sloppy. If you want to hit a strip joint, we can hit a strip joint, I don't care. I'm begging you here, buddy. Please."

Half an hour later he showed up at my place — with Farah, of course.

"Dude," he said, looking more apelike than ever. "What happened to your dome?"

"Got in a fight," I said.

"What? With who?"

"A security guard at the hospital. They wanted to put my mother in the psych ward, and I said no fuckin' way."

Chad's jaw dropped. "You're shitting me."

Farah laughed and shook her head.

On the way to the bar — The Bloody Paw, where else? — I told them all about Darcy's failed attempt at rape, my unfortunate trip to the hospital, and the fucked-up visit to Gloria's cat sanctuary.

Chad soaked in these tidbits with the enthusiasm of a

teenage scandalmonger. "You could have your own reality show, dude. I'm serious."

As we turned onto Dormant Street, I bumped hard into a fat man who seemed to be in a rush. I twisted my ankle as I stumbled, and he dropped the cardboard box he was carrying. Rolls of duct tape and a bundle of rope fell to the side of the road.

"Watch where you're going, tubby," Chad said.

The man opened his mouth to say something, but before he could speak I said, "Bill?"

"Oh shit. Brandon. I didn't realize it was you." His face went red, and he bent over to pick up his things.

I told Chad and Farah I'd meet them at the bar, and went to help Bill. He was sweating like a beaver in Saudi Arabia.

"What's with the supplies?" I said.

"Nothing. Just fixing some things around the apartment, that's all."

"Well, let me know if you need any help."

"Sure thing. By the way, I heard about your leave of absence. I'm sorry, Brandon. I can't say I didn't warn you, though. Dick's had his eye on you for weeks." He looked me in the face for the first time. "Hey, what happened to —"

"Had a little accident. It's fine."

He stood up with his box of things and I tossed in the last roll of tape.

"I'm kind of in a rush here, otherwise I'd buy you a beer or something. But give me a call, Brandon, okay? Hang in there."

"You got it, Bill."

I watched him waddle down the street, the waist of his workpants slipping farther down his ass with every step.

I checked myself out in a few store windows as I limped the rest of the way to the bar. I looked like an escaped mental patient. I didn't care. My appearance mirrored my state of mind, and there was something invigorating about that. Something primal and threatening. I was in the mood to be threatening.

There was the usual cluster of smokers standing outside The Bloody Paw. The music was louder than usual. I could hear it from the end of the block. Chad and Farah emerged from the crowd, spotted me, and jogged to meet me.

"Why don't we go somewhere else? I'm sick of this place," said Chad, the master of subtlety and persuasion. Farah stood beside him with her shoulders hunched, nodding rapidly.

"Why? What's the matter?"

"Come on." He spun me around. "Half-price pints at, umm . . ."

I pulled away. "Don't touch me. I want a fucking beer, and I want to drink it at that shithole right there. You can come or not, I really don't care at this point."

I made for the crowd. They didn't follow me. Joan Jett's "I Hate Myself for Loving You" blasted through the speakers and out onto the streets. Everyone outside the bar seemed to be looking inside, and everyone inside seemed to be cheering. I nudged my way to the window, but it was fogged up. All I could see was a blurry mass of bodies. On my way to the door, someone's lit cigarette burned my arm, and a fat guy stepped on my foot — the foot with the twisted ankle.

Someone said, "Watch it, gimp!"

I went inside. There was a banner hanging above the bar:

Save the Bears Fundraiser Night

The tables had been rearranged to make room for a stage, and what I saw on that stage was like a hallucination. Viktor Lozowsky sat on a throne-like chair dressed in a fuzzy bear or gorilla costume with the head off. On stage in front of him, Melanie wound herself around a stripper pole, completely topless in a black G-string, while another girl held a collection bucket out to the audience. Melanie danced over to Viktor and began writhing on his fuzzy lap like a professional. He groped her ass with his paws and the crowd poured money into the bucket.

No boyfriend, no bra, no shame.

I turned around, calm as a criminal, and went home to get my baseball bat.

A quick story about good old Red Hot:

When I was twelve, my dad and I went to a father–son picnic with a few of his electrician buddies and their sons. We played a game of baseball in the afternoon, then cooked hamburgers and hot dogs on an old charcoal barbecue in the sun. As usual, dad torpedoed himself with drink. After dusk had settled in, a curious raccoon started hanging around our camp, sniffing around for crumbs and meat scraps.

For some reason, my father had it in for the little creature, calling it a good-for-nothing trash bandit, a scum scavenger, a fluffball of disease. Some of the other fathers tried to calm him down, but it only made things worse. He started throwing rocks and hot coals at it. When the raccoon snuck up behind me and stole a hot dog right from my paper plate, my dad picked up Red Hot, chased the animal into the woods, and bludgeoned its brains to slop.

Someone called the police and had my father arrested for cruelty to animals, but to no purpose. Dad said the four nights he spent in jail for the 'coon incident were four of the most restful nights of his life — and the food wasn't bad either.

My point is this: Red Hot was a killer. I took it out of my closet and gripped it tightly in my right hand. It seemed to vibrate of its own accord. It was a killer, all right.

I had no idea what I was going to do, but I left my apartment with the bat in my hand and dragged my twisted ankle back to The Bloody Paw.

Melanie was no longer on stage. The new act was some acoustic folk-punk band performing Billy Bragg covers with their shirts off and letters painted on their chests that should have spelled B-E-A-R-S had they been standing in the right order. It seemed bare chests were the theme of the night. Come to think of it, it's only *now* that I see what they were up to with the bear/ bare thing. If I'd known at the time, maybe I wouldn't have smashed up the place.

Before I did that, though, I wandered through the crowd in search of Melanie, gripping Red Hot so tightly in my hand that it became an extension of my arm. Nobody seemed to notice me. I looked like the last man standing at the end of a horror film — the one whose vengeful thirst for blood has finally matched the killer's.

One of the idiots in the crowd said to me, "I'm loving the statement, man. Powerful."

I found Melanie in the storage room with a belt tied around her arm, a needle and burnt spoon on the floor at her side. Her head was resting on a stack of flattened cardboard boxes. She was still topless, but she'd put jeans on. Her skin was glossy, almost slimy with sweat. Cradled in her arms were the pink pumps she'd worn on our first date. She rolled her head and looked at me with zero recognition on her face.

"Heavy," she said. "Heavy like a balloon."

The desire to smash things left me. I wanted to lay her over my shoulder and carry her back to my place, nurse her back to health. I was about to do just that when a voice behind me said, "Mind telling me what you're doing in my bar with a baseball bat?"

I turned. Standing in front of me was Viktor. He was still in the mascot suit.

I stepped toward him. "Mind telling me what the fuck my girlfriend is doing shooting heroin in the back room of this dump?"

"I'm sorry, did you say 'girlfriend'?" He laughed. "Get the fuck out of my bar."

"I'm taking her with me."

He put his hand on my shoulder to stop me. I was about to spin around and slug him when Melanie mumbled, "Viktor, where are you? I want you . . ."

He looked at me smugly and shrugged. "Hey. The lady has spoken."

I gritted my teeth and nodded. Kept nodding as I backed away from him. Continued to nod as I walked back into the bar. Nodded at the people in the crowd with their drinks in their hands and their parents' money in their pockets. Nodded at the band, at the bartender, at the bouncer by the door. Nodded at the dead grizzly on the wall as I wound up and shattered the half-drunk pint glasses on the table in the corner.

The music stopped. Everyone looked at me.

I took a swing at the banner and ripped it in half. I smashed table lamps and dinner plates, beer taps and bottles of wine. I would've smashed all the pictures off the wall if the bouncer hadn't chased me out of there. He couldn't run for shit. I lost him at the first turn off Dormant Street, even with my twisted ankle.

POISON SHY

When I heard the sirens I knew they'd called the cops. I took a series of shortcuts through alleyways to my mother's place, and slept on her couch with Red Hot nestled in my arms.

Morning light came through the blinds and smacked my aching eyelids, daring me to open them and face what I'd done. I half-expected my mother to be home from the hospital, frying up some bacon and eggs for her dear son, the most recent initiate into the funhouse of the disturbed. The thought was almost comforting.

Red Hot had rolled off me in the night. It lay on the carpet looking small, bashful, and ashamed, like a limp dick. The orgy of violence was over.

I peeled the bandages off my head and turned on the shower. Bits of glass fell out of my hair. The water was like acid on my skin. The thought of getting the hell out of town crossed my mind, but where was I going to go? The streets of Toronto? The ice caps of Baffin Island?

No. I had no choice but to go home, stick out my chin, and eat my demons alive.

When I saw Detective Darvish on the bench outside the laundromat, it was too late to make a run for it. He sat with his legs crossed and a tiny cup of espresso in his gigantic hand. His suit was old, his tie was pink; his loafers were about to fall apart. He looked at me with his bulbous eyes and offered a big smile.

"Mr. Galloway." He stood up. "Welcome home."

"Do you mind if I get changed first? I've been wearing these clothes for two days."

He wrinkled his brow. "First?"

"I'm not resisting arrest. I trashed the bar and I'll accept responsibility for it. But if I'm going to be put in a cell I want to at least be comfortable."

"Why would you be put in a cell?"

"I told you. For trashing The Bloody Paw. Disturbing the peace or whatever."

"I wasn't aware of any bar being trashed. But thanks for letting me know."

"Huh?"

He moved toward me. I could smell his cologne and his rank coffee breath. "I came here to investigate another matter, Mr. Galloway. We'll have to discuss the bar another time. Can I see your apartment?"

"What do you mean, another matter?"

"Let's go upstairs."

I fumbled with my keys and led him up the staircase. He walked right behind me. Stepped on my heel at one point. I opened the door at the top.

"I still don't —"

He brushed past me and went inside. "Is this it? There's no bedroom?"

"Nope. I sleep on a pull-out. Just a bathroom here and a closet over there. Sorry about the mess in the kitchen."

He looked around. Opened the closet and looked upwards, downwards. Picked up my vial of antibiotics and read the label. Went into the bathroom and looked behind the shower curtain.

"There's no storage room in this building that you'd have access to?"

"This is all I got. Do you mind telling me what this is about?"

"A girl has been reported missing. Your friend Melanie Blaxley."

"What?" I felt around for somewhere to sit.

"I received the call about . . ." He checked his watch. "About fourteen hours ago. It's not officially a missing persons case yet, but I thought I'd get a jump on things."

"What do you mean, she's missing?"

"I mean just that, sir."

"Who reported it?"

"Your other pal. Darcy Sands."

I felt a huge sense of relief. "With all due respect, Detective," I said, laughing, "I think you're being messed with. Melanie and Darcy are a couple of con artists."

"That's possible," he said. "But I'm prone to gut feelings."

"You thought I was hiding her here?"

"I've got to rule out everything."

"I'm telling you, Detective. Melanie's not missing. It's probably some sick prank. I'll give you her cell phone number if you want."

"That would be helpful, thank you."

I wrote it down and gave it to him. On his way out the door he turned to me and said, "I think I'll head over to that bar you mentioned earlier. Maybe they know something. Goodbye."

I tried Melanie's cell as soon as Darvish was gone. It rang twice, then a voice told me the customer was not available. I tried her apartment and Darcy picked up.

"Where the fuck is she?" he said, as soon as he heard my voice.

"Stop trying to land me in jail, all right? The joke's over, and it's not all that funny."

"I'm serious, Brandon. You honestly don't know where she is?"

It was the first time I'd actually heard fear in his voice. It was also, I believe, the first time he'd used my name instead of calling me *buddy* or *Bug Man*. Did he know we shared a father? I swallowed and it stung my throat.

"You there?" he said.

"I don't understand why you're worried. You know Melanie better than I do. She's probably naked and out cold in some dude's bed right now. You know I saw her shooting up last night? She's probably with Viktor. She was all over him at the bar."

"You're kidding me."

I couldn't help but laugh at how unlike himself he seemed. "What's wrong, man? This is Melanie we're talking about, isn't it? Come on."

"You don't understand. We were supposed to take off for the Dominican this morning. Our plane tickets were waiting for us at the airport in Toronto. Our flight left at six a.m. I knew she was going out last night, but she promised she'd be home by three. When she didn't show, I went looking for her. The Bloody Paw looked like it had been firebombed. I snuck in through the back door and looked around, but the place was empty. I went to her work, called all of her friends. I even called her parents, man. Nobody knows where she is. Some people saw her at the bar but said she disappeared around midnight. I figured she was with you, even though she promised she was done with your ass. I went to your apartment but she wasn't there, and neither were you."

"Wait. You broke into my place *again*?"

"What would you have done?"

He had me there. I didn't know *what* I would have done. What did I know about what I was capable of anymore?

"I didn't even think of Viktor," Darcy went on. "I'm an idiot. She probably *is* with that necromancer. I better call that cop back."

"What cop?"

"That Paki who arrested us the other night. When I called the station to report Melanie missing, he's the one who showed up at my door fifteen minutes later. He probably thought it was a scam. Anyway, I gotta go." He hung up.

It seemed I had two options: wait around for Darvish to come back and arrest me for trashing the bar, or get out there, find Melanie, and figure out what the fuck was going on. What did I have to lose but everything? Which, in my case, wasn't much at all.

The teenager behind the counter at Darryl's Doughnuts said Melanie had taken the week off to go on vacation, she couldn't remember where. I didn't have a key to Melanie's apartment, and there was no way I could show my face at The Bloody Paw. I tried to find Viktor Lozowsky in the phone book but he wasn't listed. Was I out of options already?

I went to a pay phone and tried Melanie's cell again. This time it didn't even ring. All I got was a fast busy signal. Maybe she didn't want to be found.

I hung up and dialled the number for The Bloody Paw without a plan of any sort. It rang fourteen times — I counted — before someone picked up. Whoever it was didn't say anything. There was dead air between us for a good ten seconds. Who was I not talking to? Who was I to them?

Finally, a voice said, slowly, "Is something wrong?"

I flexed my throat muscles and said, "I was just wondering what time you'll be opening tonight."

"Who is this?" was the reply. "Where are you calling from?"

I fumbled with the receiver and hung up. I was pretty sure I'd just spoken to Viktor, but it was hard to tell. What did he mean, "Is something wrong?" Had Darvish been to see him? If so, I was probably being hunted. I had to be on the move. No doubt there were a couple of tough cops waiting to arrest me if I went back home. I considered going to my mother's place, but that seemed risky too. I almost dialled Chad, then checked myself. Darvish could've gotten to him through Farah.

There was no doubt about it — I was totally alone. So I did what all loners do in desperate circumstances: I sought out another loner.

Bill lived in a square building on a street that was more like an alleyway, just off Dormant Street, where the string of campus bars ended and the row of fabric shops and greasy breakfast diners began. I'd dropped him off a few times after work, when it was my turn to have the truck, but he'd never invited me in. Bill wasn't the inviting type.

There was a skinny bald guy with a red goatee leaning against the side of the building. He had a handkerchief tied around his neck and his shirt was unbuttoned.

"BBBJ?" he mumbled, as I walked past.

I pretended I didn't hear him and went inside. The tenants' names and apartment numbers were scribbled on a sheet that was tacked to a chewed-up corkboard on the wall. There were no buzzers. Anyone could just walk in off the street, find your number, and break down your door.

I looked at the sheet of tenants. *Bill Barber — 210*. I thought, *Beer-guzzling Bill Barber, the Bug guy, with the Big gut, Bad gas, and Boring life*. His name suited him just fine.

I didn't trust the elevator so I took the stairs. 210 was at the end of the hall. As I approached the door, I heard some music coming from inside that sounded like Britney Spears. Maybe the apartment numbers on the sheet were wrong. I knocked anyway.

Nobody came, so I knocked a little louder. "Hey Bill, you there? It's Brandon."

The music shut off. There was some shuffling around, the screech of duct tape, and then a door slammed. Whoever was in there was panting so loudly I could hear their breath from my side of the door. It was a familiar wheeze. Bill opened the door.

He tried to smile, but he couldn't hide his surprise. His face was purple as an eggplant, and there was an expensive-looking camera hanging around his neck.

"Brandon, what are you doing here?"

"You okay, Bill? You look a little flushed."

"I'm fine. What's the matter?"

"Can I come in? I'm in a bit of a jam."

He moved to block more of the doorway. "Now's not a good time."

I laughed. "Why? You too busy dancing to Britney Spears or something? Taking pictures of yourself? Don't worry Bill, I won't tell anyone."

"Seriously, Brandon. You can't come in."

"Come on, Bill. Why not? I need you to do me this favour."

He turned his head, looked back into his apartment, then turned to face me again. "I've got a girl in here, okay? A hooker. You get me?"

Embarrassed, I looked down at the collection of boots and shoes inside Bill's door. "Sorry, Bill. I didn't realize. Sorry."

"Take it easy, Brandon," he said, and shut the door.

I walked out of the building, ignoring the gigolo outside for a second time, and hurried straight for home. Hopefully Darvish was there waiting for me, so I could tell him I'd seen Melanie's pink pumps inside Bill's apartment.

The cops were waiting for me, just like I knew they'd be — two mustachioed bruisers who looked like they'd tasted blood before and liked it.

They were too busy imagining who had the bigger dick to notice me coming.

"Officers," I called as I hustled toward them.

One of them hit the other on the shoulder and nodded at me.

I put my hands in the air. "I need to talk to Detective Darvish."

"Stop," said the thicker of the two. "Don't fuckin' move another step."

I stopped. "Where's Darvish? I need to —"

They threw me against the window of the laundromat. There was an old lady inside who went on folding her clothes despite the commotion.

"Spread 'em!"

The side of my face was pressed so hard against the glass it was hard to speak. I tried to say, "I know where the girl is," but it came out like slurred German. They frisked me, cuffed me, read me my rights. Threw me head first into the back of their squad car. I said, "I'm telling you, I need to talk to Darvish *now*!" They slammed the door in my face.

One of them pulled out a walkie-talkie and spoke into it. I tried to read his lips but couldn't. Who else would they be calling but Darvish?

I knocked on the window with my forehead. "Hey! Tell him I know where Melanie is!"

The idiot without the walkie-talkie pointed at me. I read his lips: "Shut. Up."

What did I expect from a couple of Frayne cops? I tried to calm down. I could explain everything to Darvish when he showed up. I sat and wondered how Melanie could have ended up at Bill's. Did a pair of pink pumps even mean anything? Maybe Bill liked to cross-dress. But no, they were way too small for him.

I started second-guessing myself. I couldn't help but wonder if this was all an elaborate prank. Was everyone conspiring against me, even the cops? My mother always said that law enforcement was blasphemous, a rebellion against Divine Law. My father just said cops were nothing but crooked criminals. Maybe I should have listened.

The two officers sat down on the bench. I made eye contact with one of them and gave him a pleading look. He spat and turned away.

Where the fuck was Darvish?

Ten minutes later, he pulled up in a busted old Chrysler. He shook his thugs' hands, got into the squad car's passenger seat, and looked at me through the rear-view mirror.

"Nice work at the bar," he said. "You could have been a pro ballplayer."

"I know where Melanie is," I said. "She's at a man named Bill Barber's place on Falk, just off Dormant. I don't know if she's being held against her will. You have to go there."

"I don't have to do anything but take you to the station."

"What? What about Melanie? I thought she was your priority. Let those guys take me in, I don't care. Just go to Bill Barber's, I'm telling you."

"And what makes you think that, Mr. Galloway?"

"I saw her shoes. I saw her pink pumps in his doorway."

"When was this?"

"I don't know. About half an hour ago."

"And who is Bill Barber?"

"I work with him. He's my supervisor."

He wrote something down on a little notepad and stuck it in his pocket. "Mr. Lozowsky told me a different story. He says Miss Blaxley's on her way to see her parents in Stittsville. Said he drove her to the bus depot this morning."

"What?"

"How do you know the shoes you saw were Miss Blaxley's?"

"Well, I don't know for sure."

He pulled a napkin out of his pocket and blew his nose. "I'm going to have my men bring you to the station. I'm sure you'll cooperate. I apologize if they were a little rough."

I said, "Wait!" but he got out of the car and slammed the door. Said something to his apes, got back into his own car, and drove off.

As I was being escorted to the station, one of the bruisers farted. I held my breath and looked out the window. The sky was grey as smoke, and my stomach was starting to turn.

I managed to swallow down the first rush of bile, but the taste was too much. The second retch was a projectile, aimed straight at the back of Tweedle Dee's fat neck.

"What the *fuck*?" he said, my puke dripping down his collar.

Tweedle Dum, the driver, craned to look at me. "Fuck," he said. "He's white as a goddamn sheet."

My groan was drowned out by the horn of another car. Tweedle Dum, still looking back at me, had veered onto the wrong side of the road. He was headed straight for a parked car. I ducked, the only one prepared for impact.

I didn't see what happened up front, but I definitely heard it. Metal on metal, shattered glass, ribcages thumping against dashboard, the bang and hiss of airbags and exhaust. The two cops groaning as they struggled to suck in air. And then, the miracle: the back door popped open with the quietest of clicks. A real life *deus ex machina*.

I peeked up front. The driver was out behind the steering wheel, facing away from me. His partner was slumped awkwardly toward the passenger-side floor, dazed, wincing, and holding his chest. Neither of them had been wearing a seatbelt.

Without a second thought, I pushed my door open with my foot, crawled out, and took off down the street with my hands cuffed behind me. I stumbled, fell. Got up and continued running, quickly but carefully. I ran like an ostrich, on my toes, with long bounding strides.

I headed to Bill's a fugitive.

People on the streets saw the handcuffed lunatic sprinting by in a puke-stained shirt with blood-crusted hair, but they didn't say a word. They ignored me. For all they knew, I was homicidal — and I might have been. The truth was that I didn't know myself anymore, but it was a good feeling, like I'd been suffocating in a shell my whole life and had only now chipped my way out into a realm that was familiar but unpredictable.

For the first time in my life I knew I was capable of surprising myself.

I turned onto Bill's block and stopped to catch my breath. Darvish's Chrysler was parked across from the apartment building. I walked over and touched my knuckles to the hood. It was still hot.

The bald guy with the handkerchief and red goatee was still hanging around outside. "Ooh, I love the handcuffs," he said. "Very kinky. If you're looking for your boyfriend, he went inside."

I was tired as hell of prostitutes. I shot him a fuck-you glare and made for the front door. Turned around and tried to open it with my cuffed hands. No go. Through the glass I could see Darvish walking down the hall to the elevator.

Mr. Goatee Man approached me. "Need some help there, trooper?"

He put his bony hand on my shoulder, and as he did so, a scream, hoarse and desperate and female, stabbed through the air like a knife from the rooms upstairs. I looked into Goatee

Man's eyes and saw my fear reflected in them. He opened the door and I ran inside. The elevator doors had just closed with Darvish inside. I took the stairs. When I reached the second floor I stumbled and fell. Someone grabbed the back of my shirt and hauled me up. It was Darvish. His finger was pressed against his lips. I nodded, terrified.

There was a gun in his hand, a cold black piece of steel. He'd become the Grim Reaper in a sweater vest and chalky slacks. He dug his free hand into his pocket, pulled something out, and yanked me by the collar. For a second I thought he was going to stick me with a sedative; instead he reached down and unlocked my cuffs. Then he turned around and walked slowly in the direction of 210, the apartment from which the scream had come. Bill's apartment.

I started to follow, but he stuck his arm out to stop me. Shook his head no without turning around.

I leaned against the wall and slid into a sitting position. There wasn't anything to do but wait for death — mine or someone else's. There was no escaping it. It hung in the air, hot, poisonous, unavoidable. The scary thing was that I wanted to see it happen. I wanted to watch life disappear from someone's eyes. Did that make me a psychopath?

Darvish stood flat against the wall outside Bill's door with his gun in the air. "This is the police," he said, loudly. "Open the door and put your hands in the air."

"*Help me!*" someone screamed. A girl. "*Oh God, please help me!*"

"I'm coming in," Darvish called.

He took a step backward and kicked open the door. He ducked right away, aiming his gun where someone's throat would have been, had anyone been standing there.

"*Oh fuck, help me. He's hiding somewhere. Help me, please.*"

It was Melanie's voice. I stood up. Darvish swooped into the room and disappeared. I followed him.

The place smelled horrible, like rotten onions. It slapped you in the face. I put my hand to my mouth and nose.

"In here! Help me."

I followed Darvish toward Melanie's voice. He turned on his heels and pointed the gun at my face. "Get the fuck out of here!" he said in a loud whisper.

I ran past him. He tried to grab my shirt and missed. I stumbled and fell to my knees as I burst through the door at the end of the hall.

Melanie was strapped to a dirty mattress on the floor, spread-eagle and fully naked, with bear traps clamped to both her ankles, the metal teeth biting deep into her skin. One of her feet was bent to the side. Exposed bone jutted out the side of her ankle like a lamb chop. The other foot was purple with bruises. She was the palest I'd ever seen her; even her freckles had lost their colour.

She whispered, "Brandon." It was a foreign word. Everything changes in the face of human viciousness, a close-up view of pure evil. Nothing is ever the same again.

Darvish rushed into the room behind me. "Oh my God." He didn't sound like a cop then. Whatever he'd seen in his years on the beat — and something told me he'd seen a lot — the sight of Melanie shook him. His mouth was open; his gun hung loosely from his hand like a toy.

"He's still *here*," Melanie said softly, her voice half-dead.

The words seemed to jolt Darvish back into action. He raised his gun and surveyed the room while I crouched at Melanie's side and attempted to untie the ropes from her wrists. My hands were shaking. I sobbed and gagged. I thought, for some reason, of my mother in the hospital, and then of

Melanie's parents, whoever they were. The body on the mattress was their little girl.

From somewhere in the hall came the sound of slow footsteps. We all stopped — moving, breathing, everything. Darvish held his gun in both hands and aimed it at the doorway.

The steps got closer. Whoever was out there was moaning like a bereaved sea monster. It was the sound of surrender. Of accepting, even embracing, a violent fate.

Bill walked through the door, naked and shivering, his huge gut eclipsing his penis. There was a corkscrew in his hand. He pointed it feebly at Darvish. The gesture was enough: the cop's bullet hit him in the chest. Bill Barber took it willingly, almost proudly, before he crumpled to the floor and muttered, "I never did it before."

Prison was never an option. Bill Barber had to die.

I think he wanted to.

Another day, another *hour*, and Melanie could have bled out in that room, the walls of which were plastered with pornographic Polaroids that Bill had taken before strapping her to the mattress. The photographs were incredible, artistic in a way that only someone who doesn't know what they're doing can achieve, perfectly capturing Melanie's gruff sensuality. It even looked like she was enjoying herself. I guess she didn't know what was coming.

The pictures were spread around in a crude overlapping collage reminiscent of the way Melanie's own bedroom was decorated. Had Bill been stalking her since day one, as I had? The thought made me feel like an accomplice.

Still does.

Melanie was rushed directly to Saint Aiden's. I was put into the back of Darvish's Chrysler and left to watch as almost every cop, paramedic, and journalist in Frayne arrived on the scene. Yellow caution tape was unfurled. Photographs were taken. Mr. Goatee was being interviewed by two uniformed officers. It looked like he was crying.

I was still in the car when Bill's body was carried out of the building on a stretcher. He was wrapped in a body bag, his gut so big that his corpse might've been mistaken for that of a pregnant woman.

His last words echoed in my brain. *I never did it before*. Did what, Bill? Kidnapped a young girl, tied her to a filthy mattress, raped her and tortured her? Maybe it was simpler, more pathetic than that. Maybe Bill had been a virgin. There was no way of knowing.

A few minutes later, Darvish joined me in the back seat of the squad car.

"You're a crafty bastard, you know that?" he said. "I could charge you with a whole slew of things if I wanted to. Resisting arrest. Assaulting an officer. Escaping police custody. You'd get years. But you know what? I'm going to forget all that."

I stared out the window and didn't say a word.

He put his massive hand on my shoulder. "If I were you I'd get out of here. This town, I mean, when this is all over. There's nothing good here. Trust me, I know."

"My mother's in the hospital," I said. "I'd like to go see her."

He laughed. "You want me to let you go?"

I didn't say anything.

"All right," he said, reaching for his keys. "I'll drive you there."

POISON SHY

We never got to Saint Aiden's. It seems inevitable when I think back on it. Somebody else was bound to die.

We were the only car stopped at the traffic light. The town was eerily deserted. Stores were closed. Lights were off. It was 3:13 p.m.

Darvish stuck a fingernail between his teeth to dislodge a piece of food. I watched him struggle with it, trying different fingers as he attempted to dig out whatever it was. When I looked out the window, I realized we were just down the street from The Bloody Paw. I looked at the bar and thought of the pictures I'd smashed. I hadn't been able to hear anything that night. All sound had sunken into the vacuous hum of blood and adrenaline inside my head.

The light turned green. Darvish put his foot on the gas. Before we'd managed to move more than a few feet, a body smashed through the window of The Bloody Paw, skidding along the sidewalk amidst a shower of sparkling glass.

"Jesus," Darvish said as he swerved and stopped.

A second figure stepped through the broken window, wielding a barstool in both hands like a sledgehammer. It was Viktor. He was decked out in full army gear — camouflage pants and tank top, dog tag and knee-high Doc Marten boots, the works. The rag doll on the sidewalk, scraping to get away, was my half brother.

Darvish burst out of the car. "Police!" he shouted, running toward them.

Viktor walked calmly toward Darcy, then hit him as hard as he could with the stool. The seat struck his temple; Darcy's head snapped violently to one side. Viktor let go of the stool before Darvish tackled him to the ground and cuffed him.

I got out of the car and ran to Darcy's side. He was dead, no question about it. There was a crater in his head where he'd been struck, his neck was bent and slightly elongated. He was smiling, though — peacefully, his eyes wide open. There was a chain around his neck, something I'd never seen him wear before, with a crucifix on it. The stem of the cross had swung up and into Darcy's mouth.

It was the way he would've wanted to go.

Turns out it was Viktor who'd brought Melanie to Bill's. He'd had his fun with her at the bar, drugged her, and delivered on a promise he'd made to get his old pal Bill laid before his fiftieth birthday. He figured Melanie was perfect for the job. He thought she might even enjoy it. He claimed not to know what Bill had planned — but whether or not he did didn't matter. He'd killed Darcy right in front of a cop.

What happened before we got there, I can only guess — but I know it was all about Melanie. If love was something Darcy was capable of feeling, I believe he felt it for her and her alone. He and Viktor had been battling for her attention long before I got involved with her. Darcy'd gone to confront his rival, and it had ended violently, as things between men often do. Melanie did that to people. Made them lose it. I knew that first hand.

The reason Viktor gave for killing Darcy was simple, and yet, it wasn't a reason at all: "The douchebag had it coming." He wouldn't say any more. It didn't matter. Viktor's days as a civilian were over.

As for me, I was charged with disturbing the peace for my aggressive redecorating of The Bloody Paw, and slapped on the wrist with a $5,000 fine. Darvish was kind to me. He knew I'd been through my share of hell already.

There's a term in the pest control business — poison shy. It refers to when an animal or insect learns to avoid a certain toxic substance after ingesting a sublethal dose. It's a survival instinct. Nature's alarm system. It's the best analogy I have to explain why I didn't visit Melanie in the hospital.

I decided to take Darvish's advice and get out of town, maybe go back to school. I applied to every major university in Canada except for F.U. I ended up getting accepted into the concurrent education program at York University in Toronto. Thought I might try my hand at teaching. It was Darcy who told me that the students who hate school make the best teachers because they actually want to change the system, make it better. I think he was right.

In the meantime I got a job washing dishes at Parker's Grill, formerly The Jug. My first night on the job I learned that Gloria had taken a prolonged leave of absence after Darcy's death. I never worked a single shift with her and never saw her again. It was probably for the best. I saved every cent I made until it was time to leave for school.

The only person I kept in touch with was Chad, more out of obligation than anything. He and Farah got more serious by the day, building toward a semi-normal small-town life together. I became a story for them to tell other couples, their connection to that famous day of violence in Frayne. Eventually I'd be reduced to a footnote in a dinner party conversation, a side character in a creepy local history that would one day become legend.

At school I kept my distance from my classmates. I was the loner at the back of the lecture hall, not quite a mature student but too old to get invited to parties. I got the grades I needed to pass and faded into the background. It was my old life all over again. It was the most comfortable I'd felt in a long time.

On weekends I'd hop on the subway line and explore the city. I appreciated the anonymity. Everyone inwardly plunging into their own secret obsessions and personal nightmares. It was a soothing thought to someone like me. Nobody, except maybe monks and retards, is ever truly happy. The city helped me realize that. I was just another suffering dog.

One of my ventures took me to Greektown in the east end. I went to a café and did some reading for school, then stopped at one of the dozens of Mediterranean restaurants for lunch. The place was empty. As I perused the menu, the waitress came over to take my drink order. Without looking up, I asked for a Bloody Caesar. The waitress stood there and didn't respond, and when I looked up at her I realized why. It was Patricia Moreno.

"I can't believe it," she said. "You look exactly the same."

I laughed. I didn't *feel* exactly the same. As for Patricia, she was fat. She'd always been a bit bulky, but never this big. She didn't look bad, though. There was still something sexy about her, in a rap music video kind of way.

"I thought you moved to Montreal," I said.

"I was there for a bit," she said. "I also lived in Calgary, Saskatoon, Winnipeg, and St. John. I moved to Toronto with a guy I was seeing, but it didn't last. I guess the fat chick thing got old. His loss. And *what* a loss!"

I'd forgotten about her self-deprecating sense of humour.

"Sit down," I said. "Have lunch with me. Let's catch up."

She looked toward the kitchen. "I better not. My boss is the biggest asshole. I'm off at five, though, if you want to get a drink."

I thought it over as I ate my souvlaki. Why shouldn't I have drinks with Patricia? It didn't have to mean anything. I just hoped she didn't want to have sex. I'd been experiencing erectile difficulties since leaving Frayne. I couldn't even masturbate. Every time I tried, I was flooded with images of Melanie's bruised and mangled body. The idea of sex had become absurd, devoid of all intimacy and function. It was a kind of violence, degrading and potentially lethal.

Thank God for Patricia.

We got hammered at a pub and had a good laugh at Frayne's expense. We called it a pasture of shite, Satan's colon, a third-rate trash hole, the incest hub o' the world. She brought me back to her place and went down on me in her building's stairwell. I think one of her neighbours saw us.

My penis worked.

It was a small miracle.

I conducted my requisite volunteer hours at an elementary school called Precious Blood. I was placed in Mrs. Thurber's grade three class. Mrs. Thurber didn't seem to want me there. She dominated the classroom with her horn-rimmed glasses and thirty-inch pointer, a threat she'd wield like a fencing blade. She referred to me dismissively as "Brendan" or "Mr. Gilroy."

I sat at the back of the classroom in a metal fold-up chair and kept my mouth shut most of the time. The kids seemed terrified of having a strange man who never said a word looming behind them all day. Who could blame them?

There was one kid, a loner named Justin, who sat in the back corner and paid no attention to Mrs. Thurber or any of his peers. He spent most of the day drawing pictures of robots and monsters in his notebook. He seemed to sense that I was just as bored as he was. One day he started holding up his drawings for me to see. They were done in comic-book style, with an attention to detail that was quite impressive for an eight-year-old.

I gave him the thumbs up. He smiled and started on a new one.

It made me feel that my life was moving in the right direction.

During my second month of school, I got a call from a Dr. Zimmerman from the psych ward at Saint Aiden's. My mother had passed away in her sleep from what stymied medical professionals refer to as "natural causes." She was sixty-one years old.

I took a Greyhound back to Frayne the next weekend, picked up her ashes, and took the next available bus back to York. There was no point in a funeral. Who would have gone?

It was Patricia who told me to give my mother the send-off she would have wanted.

"What kind of send-off would she have wanted?" I asked.

"She was your mother, Brandon. You tell me."

I let my mother's ashes sit on my desk for a week. I thought about the state of constant fear in which she'd lived most of her life, and how that was all over. I thought about the ninety-nine percent of me that didn't believe in the absurdity of an afterlife, and how the one percent that did hoped there was a place in heaven for people like my mother. Perhaps the simple fact that she no longer existed, and therefore would no longer suffer, was heaven enough.

I took a bus back to Frayne. Booked a room in a motel, a brand new Super 8 that had been under construction when I'd left. The room smelled like fresh paint.

On Friday night I prowled the graveyard and visited Darcy's headstone. The inscription was the same as what he'd scrawled on his bedroom door in permanent marker: the Oscar Wilde quip, "The truth is rarely pure and never simple." I placed two twigs over his grave and made a crucifix out of them, then stomped on it with my heel, crunching it into bits. A crude cross shape remained. It seemed like the kind of thing Darcy would have appreciated.

On Saturday I went to church. I brought my mother's urn with me.

POISON SHY

The pews were mostly empty save a few lonely worshippers, all of them women. I went up to the balcony and looked at the stained-glass windows, then down at the deserted altar. The building hummed. One of the worshippers lit a candle in front of a statue of Mary and left.

I looked up at the ceiling. Six or seven giant fans hung from the rafters, spinning silently as though propelled by sacred air.

I took the lid off my mother's urn and stood up. There was one person left in the church, a middle-aged woman in the second row. I held my breath and flung my mother's ashes upward into the swirl of the fans, again and again, until the urn was empty. A cloud of black dust spread and fell among the pews. The woman did nothing and continued to pray as if all was well. As if, in a world presided over by God, a shower of ashes was a blessing to be ignored.

My bus back to Toronto was leaving on Sunday morning. I didn't feel like sitting around my motel room and coating my lungs with paint fumes, so I decided to take a walk around town, revisit some old haunts.

I felt good, like I'd really accomplished something meaningful at the church, though I didn't fully understand why.

There was a cop car parked in the lot outside Darryl's Doughnuts. I went inside, thinking I might find Darvish or one of his lackeys. It turned out to be a fat patrolman who looked exactly like Bill Barber. I ordered a coffee and a Boston cream doughnut and stared at Bill's lookalike as I ate and drank. He didn't look at me once, just chatted with the teenaged girl behind the counter. She kept asking to see his badge like she didn't believe he was a real cop. I wasn't sure I believed him either.

Afterwards I went to visit my old apartment. I stood on

the street outside and stared up at the window above the laundromat. The new tenant had put up leopard-print curtains, and there was a half-drunk bottle of gin on the windowsill. For some reason it occurred to me that a prostitute might live there. I hoped it wasn't Melanie. I didn't press the buzzer to find out.

The windows of The Bloody Paw were covered in newsprint. The place had been shut down. I tried to peek through a torn piece of newspaper, but I couldn't see anything. It was black inside. An abyss. I wondered what had become of all the hunting pictures, the ones I hadn't managed to destroy.

I remembered reading in the *Toronto Star* that Viktor Lozowsky, kidnapper and murderer, had been transferred to Kingston Penitentiary, a maximum security prison in Ontario. He'd probably be back on the streets in a couple of years — if he survived being sodomized on a nightly basis by a six-foot-eight goliath I hoped was named Darcy.

The last place I went to was my mother's old building. I wondered if Red Hot was somewhere inside. Perhaps it had found its way to some kid's equipment bag, some future pro-leaguer who would use it to hit his first home run.

In the distance I saw someone with blazing red hair on a bench outside a bus stop, feeding bread crumbs to a flock of pigeons. It was Melanie. There were two forearm crutches propped against the bench beside her. I could hear the pigeons cooing from where I stood: a warbling chorus of hungry birds.

I looked at her for a long time. She seemed like a different person than the wildcat I'd known. She wasn't just some girl — she was a woman, a real woman, and here she was, very much alive, feeding birds and smiling down at them, because there was still beauty in the world despite all the bad things that can happen, and *she* was a part of that beauty.

After a while, she stood up and fastened the crutches to her

POISON
SHY arms. The pigeons waddled around her feet like a single entity, some of them fluttering a few feet off the ground before landing again.

She threw one last handful of crumbs in the air. The pigeons burst after them like a feathered wave. She hobbled down the street, away from me, in the direction of my mother's old building. I wanted to run after her. I wanted to look at her face and see forgiveness in it. I wanted her to know that she'd changed my life forever.

But I didn't follow her. Not this time.

ACKNOWLEDGEMENTS

I don't deserve the support and assistance I received from the following people:

Michael Holmes
Russell Smith
Andrew Pyper
Amanda Wetmore
Jowita Bydlowska
Sarah Dunn
Erin Creasey
Jake Howell
David Gee
Cat London
Matthew Firth
Sarah Gardner Borden
Everyone at ECW Press
Everyone involved in the Creative Writing MFA program at the University of Guelph

At ECW Press, we want you to enjoy this book in whatever format you like, whenever you like. Leave your print book at home and take the eBook to go! Purchase the print edition and receive the eBook free. Just send an email to ebook@ecwpress.com and include:

- the book title
- the name of the store where you purchased it
- your receipt number
- your preference of file type: PDF or ePub?

Get the eBook free!*
*proof of purchase required

A real person will respond to your email with your eBook attached. And thanks for supporting an independently owned Canadian publisher with your purchase!